BARRY SQUIRES, FULL TILT

BARRY SQUIRES, FULL TILT

HEATHER SMITH

Leabharlanna Chathair Bhaile Átha Cliath
Dublin City Libraries

PENGUIN TEEN
an imprint of Penguin Random House Canada Young Readers,
a Penguin Random House Company

Published in hardcover by Penguin Teen, 2020

1 2 3 4 5 6 7 8 9 10

Text copyright © 2020 by Heather Smith
Book design: Emma Dolan
Cover design and illustration by Emma Dolan

Manufactured in Canada

Library and Archives Canada Cataloguing in Publication

Title: Barry Squires, full tilt / Heather Smith.
Names: Smith, Heather, 1968- author.
Identifiers: Canadiana (print) 2019018857X | Canadiana (ebook) 20190188588 |
ISBN 9780735267466 (hardcover) | ISBN 9780735267473 (EPUB)
Classification: LCC PS8637.M5623 B37 2020 | DDC jC813/.6—dc23

Library of Congress Control Number: 2019950471

www.penguinrandomhouse.ca

Penguin
Random House
PENGUIN TEEN CANADA

To the real Big Gord, who taught me to just get on with it.
And, always, to Rob.

PROLOGUE

If this were my memoir, it'd probably begin with *It all started at the bingo hall.* There'd be a picture of me on the cover, my heels clicked together in midair, and on the back there'd be a blurb from Pope John Paul II saying, "The best damn book I've read since the Bible." The title would be *All Tapped Out* and underneath, instead of *by Barry Squires*, it'd say *Written with passion by Finbar T. Squires*, in honor of Nanny Squires, because she was dramatic like that.

But this isn't a memoir. Memoirs are for people who've lived long, amazing lives and have inspirational stories to tell. All I did was follow my dream of becoming a Full Tilt Dancer. And that went tits up pretty quick.

CHAPTER ONE

I'd seen the Full Tilt Dancers perform a thousand times, but it wasn't until the opening of Frankie McCall's Bingo Hall that I wanted to be one of them. Maybe it was how their tartan uniforms glowed under the neon sign. Maybe it was how their shoes clacked on the large piece of plywood Frankie had put down on the pavement. More likely, though, it was because I'd spent the last year getting kicked out of every club and extracurricular activity I'd joined, and Nanny Squires said that if I didn't find an outlet for that temper of mine, I'd have a heart attack by the time I was twenty.

The parking lot in front of the hall had been cordoned off for the performance. Mom stood behind me with her hands on my shoulders while Dad, the good son that he was, brought Nan to the front to find a chair. I wished my baby brother, Gord, was there because he'd have loved the traditional Newfoundland music, but he was home with our older sister, Shelagh, who'd stayed behind to clear up after our big Sunday lunch. My other brother, Pius, wasn't impressed. "Stop being a saint, will ya?" he'd said. "You're making the rest of us look bad." Pius, or Sweet Sixteen, as Mom had been calling him since his birthday, had a big mouth and a comment for everything. When he'd heard that we were going to see the Full Tilt Dancers, he'd said, "Irish step dancing's for tools." As I stood in the crowded parking lot, mesmerized by the frenetic movements of the troupe, I felt like our Black and Decker 400-watt variable-speed jigsaw. Because if step dancing was for tools, I was the biggest one in the shed.

Frankie McCall stood under his bright neon sign tapping his foot and clapping his hands.

"Look at him," said Mom. "He's like the cat that ate the canary."

The Full Tilt Dancers had been scheduled to perform at the One Step Closer to God Nursing Home, but McCall had lured them away with the promise of five free bingo games per person. Father O'Flaherty's Full Tilt Dancers were the most sought-after act in the city—with the popular bagpiper Alfie Bragg and His Agony Bag being a close second.

The bingo fanatics of St. John's had been thrilled to learn that Frankie McCall was building a new bingo hall. The parish hall, where the game was normally played, had a rat problem. Nan blamed the infestation on the Hawkins Cheezies that were sold at the snack bar. "Finding one of those on the ground is like striking gold for a rat," she'd said. I agreed. I'd been known to eat a few off the floor myself.

Bingo attendance at the parish hall had diminished and when the town blabbermouth, Bernadette Ryan, called in to the VOCM *Open Line* radio show to say that her ninety-nine-year-old bingo-loving grandmother was showing signs of the plague—runny nose, fatigue, weakness—people refused to go altogether. Our old parish priest, Father Molloy, tried to reason with his parishioners, saying that the place had been fumigated, not once but twice, but Bernadette would not be silenced. She said that fumigation wasn't enough, that during the Great Plague of London contaminated bedding and clothes were burned to avoid contagion; therefore, the rat-infested parish hall should be burned to the ground. That's when Frankie McCall stepped in with the news that he'd be building a new bingo hall on behalf of the church. On the day of the announcement,

Father Molloy called McCall a "great philanthropist." Mom said, "Philanderer, more like." When I asked what that meant, she told me to go ask my Aunt Tilly. As far as I knew, I didn't have one.

After the dancers' opening performance, Frankie gestured to the double doors, which were blocked off by a piece of yellow police tape.

"That's what you get," said Frankie, "when you leave the village idiot in charge of the ribbon cutting."

The "village idiot" was ninety-four and Frankie's mother. I sidled up to her. "That son of yours is a hard ticket."

"Don't worry," she said. "He'll get his comeuppance."

Frankie made a cutting motion with his fingers. "Where are the scissors?"

The village idiot passed him a pair of pink plastic safety scissors. I laughed my arse off and said, "Nice one, missus."

Frankie broke a sweat as he hacked through the tape. On the final snip, the Full Tilt Dancers did a celebratory step dance. The dancing was good but "I'se da B'y" was too obvious. If it were up to me, we'd have sung "Bingo." *There was a Frankie had a hall, and BINGO was the game-o. B-I-N-G-O.* Clearly this troupe needed my out-of-the box ideas. When the applause faded I told my parents that my new life goal was to become a Full Tilt step dancer.

"Not a chance," said Dad. "We'll be drove nuts with the racket."

"But I have a feeling," I said. "It's stirring deep in my loins."

"For goodness sake, Barry," whispered Mom. "You should never talk about your loins in the shadow of the basilica."

"You just made that up," I said. "They talk about loins in the Bible all the time."

Dad ushered us toward the hall. "Come on. Bingo's starting."

"Bingo shmingo," I said. "We're talking about my dreams here."

"The answer is no," said Mom. "You'll only quit after a few weeks anyway."

"And the last thing we need is you clicking around the house like a moron," said Dad.

I picked up a rock and lobbed it at the neon sign. "Well, screw ye all!"

The rock landed two feet short of its target.

"You're lucky you missed," said Frankie McCall. "A move like that could get your whole family banned from the hall for life."

"So help me God," said Mom, "if you screw this up for me, I'll disown you."

She loved a good game of bingo.

As we filed into the hall, Dad pulled me back by the elbow. "What the hell is wrong with you, Barry? The first time your mother leaves the house since Gord's been born and you have to turn into the Antichrist."

I yanked my arm away. "If you must know," I said, "I'm Jesus's number one fan and that, sir, makes me pro-Christ. Very pro-Christ indeed."

"Don't 'sir' me, Barry," said Dad. "I'm your father, for Christ's sake."

"Taking the Lord's name in vain," I said. "*Now* who's the Antichrist?"

I caught up to Nanny Squires, who was waiting for me at the snack bar. Every week she bought me a treat—my reward for helping her keep track of the twenty cards she played at once. "Get whatever you want," she said. As I browsed, my stomach rumbling, she added, "Except Hawkins Cheezies. They started the plague, you know."

Frankie Hall had done an outstanding job stocking the new snack bar. I was spoiled for choice! "Look, Nan," I said, "they even have May Wests." But Nan didn't respond. She was too busy marveling at the shininess of the new counter. "I hope they use Comet on this," she said. "It'll help keep the sparkle."

I picked a bag of salt and vinegar chips and we joined my parents at a crowded table.

"What's up with these cards?" I said. They were different than the ones we usually played. They didn't even have the word *bingo* written across the top.

"Frankie wants to try ninety-ball bingo," said Nan.

"He played it when he was on holiday in the UK," said Mom.

"Concentrate now, Finbar," said Nan. "There'll be no letters called, just numbers."

"This is madness," said Dad. "Pure madness."

The four of us sat with our bingo dabbers hovering over the cards, waiting for the caller to shout the numbers. The sound system crackled to life.

"Tickety-boo, sixty-two."

"What the hell?" said Dad.

Frankie McCall was standing nearby. "It's how the British do it," he said. "Doesn't it add another level of fun?"

"Cup of tea, number three."

I recognized that voice. It was Uneven Steven, the colorful Englishman who was a fixture in the downtown core.

"Dirty Gertie, number thirty."

"What a load of old foohlishness," said Mom.

"Dancing queen, seventeen."

Dad elbowed me in the ribs. "There you go, Barry. A new lucky number for ya."

The laughter at the table caused a growling deep in my belly.

"Control yourself, Fin-bear," said Mom.

My fist closed in on the bingo dabber till Nan's cards were swimming in ink.

"Look what you're after doing!" said Nan. "I was one away from four corners."

"These artistic types," said Dad. "They're so high-strung."

I punched my bag of chips.

"Chips on the floor, forty-four."

I ran outside and lobbed another rock at the sign.

"Hey, watch it!"

Billy Walsh, from ninth grade, was sitting on a concrete wall eating a feed of fish and chips. We'd hung around a bit last year, before he'd moved up to high school.

"You almost hit me," he said.

He was a year older but twice my size. I was about to say sorry when I was blinded by a light. It was warm and powerful and made me tingle all over. I squinted toward the source. It was the sun reflecting gloriously off the silver taps of his dancing shoes.

"Do you hear that?" I asked.

"Hear what?"

I smiled. The chorus of angels singing hallelujah was for my ears only. I, Barry Squires, was meant to tap for Jesus.

I hopped up onto the wall next to him. "Tell me. What do you have to do to become a Full Tilt Dancer?"

He popped a chip in his mouth. "Sell your soul to the devil."

"Fair enough," I said. "Anything else?"

He shrugged. "Sign yourself up for the auditions."

"When are the auditions?" I asked.

"September."

"That's six months away," I said. "I can't wait that long."

"Patience is a virtue, kid."

"What about the uniform?" I said. "How do I get one of those?"

"O'Flaherty sells them. A hundred and twenty-five bucks."

The uniforms were Newfoundland tartan, which was mostly green with red, yellow, and white stripes. Nan said they looked patriotic. Pius said they looked like snots.

"A hundred and twenty-five bucks?" I said. "What a rip-off."

Billy stroked his vest. "This here's quality merchandise," he said. "One hundred percent polyester."

"One hundred percent, you say?" I was impressed. My school uniform was only sixty. The rest was cotton.

Billy dipped his cod in a blob of ketchup.

"Just be warned," he said. "The life of a dancer is not all sunshine and roses and luxurious textiles. There's a lot of prejudice in this biz. Especially for us male dancers. We're totally misunderstood."

I reached over and took a chip. "Never let the bastards get you down, Walsh."

It was what Nan said to me when I was kicked out of Scouts. (Except she didn't call me Walsh.)

I hopped off the wall.

"Hey," he said as I walked away. "Were you the one who punched a hole through the confessional screen?"

"Father Molloy was way out of line. Ten Hail Marys for one little sin?"

"What was the sin?"

"Punching a hole through the classroom door."

I went down Church Hill making a clicking noise with my mouth every time my sneakers hit the pavement. When I walked in the house, Shelagh passed me the baby. "Your turn. Pius is at hockey and I'm going to MUN to study."

Ever since Shelagh got her acceptance letter to Memorial University, she'd been hanging out there as if she were a current student.

"You'd better watch out," I said. "They'll be so sick of your ugly mug, they might kick you out before you even start."

"I'll be graduating with honors in June," she said. "Trust me, this ugly mug is one they'll be happy to have."

I was due to graduate in June too. I wondered if the high school would be happy to have my ugly mug.

Gord grabbed a clump of my hair with his chubby little hand. I'd missed him at the opening of the bingo hall.

"Guess what, Gord?" I whispered. "I'm going to be a Full Tilt Dancer."

★

Sometimes, in Newfoundland, you can have four seasons in one day, so even though it was the end of March (and spring should have been on its way), I stuffed Gord in his snowsuit to keep him warm on our post-bingo afternoon jaunt. As usual, I started by naming the homeowners and house colors. "Merchant, red. Coady, white. Walling, black." It was a tradition I'd started to keep things interesting back when I wasn't allowed to take Gord off York Street. Now that we were allowed to go farther I kept it up because Gord screamed if I didn't. Sometimes I wished Gord was as flexible with his routines as he was with his body. I saw him kiss his own arse once.

"Hanrahan, green. O'Brien, blue."

"Ahhh-baaa, ahhh-daaaa, ahhh-paaa."

Only six months old and speaking in whole sentences. It was no wonder I took every opportunity to show him off. He was practically a child genius.

Part of our routine was going to Caines. If Boo wasn't busy selling smokes or dishing up his famous Jiggs Dinner, he'd sit us down and tell us a ghost story. He'd seen a headless dude on Signal Hill once. He'd come upon him on a dark and stormy night and they'd locked eyes. Locked eyes! I couldn't believe it. Sometimes Gord nodded off during Boo's stories, but as soon as we'd leave the store he'd perk right up. It was the air that did it—it was fresh and salty and went right up our noses. He'd perk up even more when I'd take him to the harbor. I'd tip his stroller over the dock and say, "Hope you can swim, Gord!" He loved that. An old woman yelled at me once. She said I was foolhardy. I said, "Take a chill pill, missus. He's got a seatbelt on."

Today, instead of going to Caines, we went back to the bingo hall. The plywood was still outside.

"Watch this, Gord!"

I copied the dance moves the Full Tilt Dancers had done earlier. The almighty racket was glorious. There was no music, so I sang.

The night that Paddy Murphy died
is a night I'll never forget.
Some of the boys got loaded drunk
and they ain't been sober yet.

I *da-da-da*-ed the bits I didn't know and when the words came back I belted them out.

Mrs. Murphy sat in the corner
pourin' out her grief,
when Kelly and his gang
came tearing down the street.
They went into an empty room
and a bottle of whiskey stole,
and kept that bottle with the corpse
to keep that whiskey cold.

"A corpse is a dead body, Gord," I explained. "The b'ys weren't really celebrating Pat Murphy's life. They just wanted an excuse to party. That's what I think anyway. I'm not one for lyrics, not really. It's the melody I like. What about you, Gord? Do you like the melody? What do you think of my dancing, Gord? Pretty good, huh? What's with your face, Gord? You're not poopin', are ya? If ya shits your pants, we'll have to go home."

Gord laughed his sweet baby belly laugh, the one that erupted for the first time two months ago when I stubbed my toe on his high chair. I'd hopped on one foot shouting "ouch, ouch, ouch!" and the *ha-ha-ha* that burst out of his body was hearty and deep. Tears had pricked my eyes— not from the pain that throbbed in my foot but from the happy pain that throbbed in my heart.

I checked Gord's bum. He hadn't pooped his pants, so we continued on to Bannerman Park. I tried stuffing him into a baby swing. "You're some fat, Gord. But don't worry, once you start walking you'll lose all that weight. Just don't go losing your cheeks, okay? That's what makes you cute. No one likes a baby with skinny cheeks."

I pushed him high. "Hold on, Gord. If you fall out and die, Mom will kill me."

The last thing I wanted to do was ruin Mom's day. After months of the baby blues, she was finally having a good one.

★

We'd been surprised to see her up before noon this morning. We were sitting around the table eating Nan's pancakes when Mom appeared. "Are you coming to church with us?" I asked.

She ruffled my hair. "I prefer to pray in the privacy of my own home, thank you very much." She stole a piece of bacon off Dad's plate.

"Hey!" he said. She bent over and gave him a kiss on the lips. He beamed. The sight of her—fully dressed and ready to take on the day—raised our spirits.

And when she'd walked out the back door with a basket of freshly laundered clothes, we couldn't help but smile. Mom lived for laundry. She measured our lives by it: "Look at the size of the underwear I had to get Barry this week—my little boy is becoming a man . . . Shelagh's certainly got a lovely figure. 36C was my size too when I was her age. They're shriveled up a bit now, mind . . . Gord's going to need to move up a size in these sleepers. I hope I can get another pair with monkeys on them, they're my favorite."

A blast of cold air had filled the house but no one said a word. Nan quietly pulled a blanket over her knees, Shelagh slipped on her dressing gown, and Dad pulled Gord's high chair out of the draft. Pius, on the other hand, strutted around in his NHL boxers. "Some Newfoundlanders you are."

We watched as Mom reached into the basket and carefully pinned our clothes to the line. She smiled at us through the open door. "It's some day on clothes."

It was a phrase meant for days when the sun was splitting the rocks, but Mom hung out clothes all year long. Sometimes they came in as stiff as a board but we didn't care. When Mom hung out clothes, she was happy. And that meant that we were happy too.

The line shrieked as Mom yanked it through the pulley.

"That line needs oiling," said Nan.

Dad gazed out the window. "It's music to my ears."

I rubbed my goose-pimply arms. "Mine too."

★

Gord and I left Bannerman Park and went back to the bingo hall, where I showed him off to a table of old biddies. Even with cigarettes hanging out of their mouths, they managed a "God love him." They were a talented bunch.

Mom frowned when she saw me. "When you're fourteen, you can take him farther. Until then I want you sticking close to home."

"I only wanted to show him the new hall," I said. "We usually only go as far as Caines."

It was a lie, of course. I took Gord everywhere. I took him to the Zellers mall once. We rode a horse for a quarter. It wasn't a real horse. Real horses neighed. This one played the *William Tell* overture.

When we got home we watched *Rugrats* until Mom came back and put Gord down for a nap. When Dad and Nan went to the kitchen for a cup of tea, I loaded the *Riverdance* video into our VCR. Dad had given it to Mom for Christmas because Mom had a thing for Michael Flatley, who was the lead dancer. He wore bolero jackets over his shirtless torso and thin headbands across his forehead. Pius said he looked like a tool. Mom said he was making a statement. "Yeah," said Pius. "'Look at me. I'm a tool.'"

In order to master the art of Irish step dancing, I

watched the video not once, but twice. I pinned my hands to my sides and did what I figured was a pretty good rendition. Every now and then I added a quick flick of a leg in the air. It seemed to be a *Riverdance* signature move. I made it my own by adding a wink. I danced in this fashion from one side of the room to the other. There was no way I could wait until September for the Full Tilt auditions. I was too good. And how could I deny the troupe what was clearly a God-given talent? It wouldn't be fair.

So that night, after one of Nan's Sunday pot roasts, I cleared the living room and gathered everyone around. I brought in an extra kitchen chair for when Mom and Dad invited Father O'Flaherty over for an encore. O'Flaherty was relatively new to town, having taken over for Father Molloy, who'd brought shame upon the Full Tilt Dancers by using money they'd earned at a competition to buy himself a rabbit fur fedora down at Chafe and Sons. Mom and Dad hadn't had the chance to have a one-on-one with Father O'Flaherty yet, so not only would I be fulfilling a dream by becoming one of his dancers, I'd be bringing people together.

When everyone was seated, I went to the back porch and taped pennies to my shoes.

"Hurry up," said Shelagh. "I've got a chemistry test tomorrow."

"And I've got a life to live," said Pius.

In a spur-of-the-moment decision, I took off my shirt and put on the faux-fur shrug that hung on the coat rack. I tied a shoelace around my forehead. With my inner Flatley successfully channeled, I clicked into the living room with my head held high.

"Jesus, Mary, and Joseph," said Mom.

Nanny beamed. "God love him."

Dad looked grief stricken.

"Look," said Pius. "It's Dorkel Fattly."

I sucked in my gut and struck a matador pose in the doorway.

The room fell quiet.

Too quiet.

Shit.

I'd forgotten the music.

Without breaking character, I shuffled toward the stereo and pressed Play with my toe.

Then I shuffled back again.

"That was smooth," said Pius.

A Celtic reel danced out of the speakers. I stayed perfectly still.

"Are you going to dance or what?" said Dad.

Didn't they know? Flatley never made an entrance till halfway through the song.

It was hard to hold my matador pose with Shelagh

huffing and Mom tutting and Pius swearing under his breath. *They'll be sorry*, I thought, *when their cold, dead hearts come to life at the sight of me soaring over the sofa.*

"Why's he just standing there?" said Shelagh.

"Because he's an idiot," said Pius.

I could feel a growling, deep inside my belly. I tried some deep breathing.

"An idiot with asthma, by the sounds of it," said Shelagh.

"Are you going to start or what?" asked Dad.

"It's not my turn," I said. "I don't come on till the other dancers leave the stage."

"What other dancers?" said Mom.

Nan looked around the room. "I see them," she said. "Their costumes are as green as the rolling hills of the Emerald Isle."

"Oh for God's sake," said Dad.

"Bah-gah!" yelled Gord.

I put my finger up to silence them. We'd reached my favorite part and I wanted to savor it. Drums rolled in like a musical snowball, the sound growing bigger and bigger as it filled the room.

In three . . .

In two . . .

In one . . .

The fiddles burst in with a frenzy and so did I.

With my hands on my hips, I leapt into the room. I spread my legs as wide as I could and thrust my chin in the air. *This'll show 'em. The bastards.*

The china cabinet shook when I landed.

"Lord dyin' Jesus," said Mom. "There goes my great-grandmother's tea set."

A clickity-click to the left.

A clackity-clack to the right.

A few spins here.

A couple of twirls there.

God, I'd picked a long song.

I put my hands on my knees and did some kind of crisscross motion with my arms.

Then I did the Charleston.

Focus, Squires, focus. What would Flatley do? I pictured him in all his shirtless glory. "You got this, Finbar," he said in my imagination. It was all that I needed. With my arms glued tight to my sides, I tapped the bejeezus out of the floor. I stared straight ahead at the soon-to-be-filled-with-Father-O'Flaherty-chair and hoped to God I had an encore in me.

I tried not to look cocky as I bowed.

Gord clapped his hands.

"Bravo, bravo!" yelled Nan.

The rest of them doubled over laughing.

"Someone call the doctor," said Shelagh. "Barry had a fit."

Pius pinged my makeshift headband as he left the room. "If I ever see you doing anything like that again, I swear to God I'll punch your face in."

I picked Gord up and slung him on my hip. The little snot-rag was the only one I could stand to be around. (Well, Nan too, but I could hardly storm off with her in my arms.)

I sat on my bedroom floor and peeled the pennies off my shoes. Gord tried to put them in his mouth. I grabbed them. "Dirty," I said. "Bah," he said back.

I stretched out on my bed with Gord on my chest. He tried to pick up my nipples.

"No, Gord. They're attached."

He reached out and touched the raised patch of purple that splashed across my cheek.

I pushed his hand away. "No!"

I felt bad. How was he supposed to know about birthmarks? I played pat-a-cake to make up for it. As I sang about the baker's man, I reflected on my performance. Maybe, instead of a live show, I should've videotaped myself, and added lots of cool edits and slo-mo in the post-production. It worked wonders in *Riverdance*. Who knows? It could've made all the difference.

★

There was something about Sunday nights that made my bedroom ceiling really interesting. Pius was in the bed next to me reading *Gretzky: An Autobiography* and I could hear *Fawlty Towers* reruns from downstairs and "Wonderwall" on repeat from Shelagh's room. I pictured Gord asleep in his cot and all around me was the smell of our Sunday supper, corned beef and cabbage, still strong in the air. Everything around me—what was in my ears and up my nose—was comforting, but Sunday nights meant Monday mornings. I stared at the bumpy texture of the ceiling. We'd had a leak the year before and the whole thing had to be redone. The painters recommended stucco because it hides imperfections, unlike the smooth surface we'd had before. They called it a popcorn ceiling but it didn't look like popcorn. It looked like crushed meringue. I thought about school the next day. Soon I'd feel like a frayed puzzle piece—no matter how hard I'd try to fit in, there'd always be bits sticking out.

I remembered that time in the dumpster. The older boys had said my face was dirty, so they chucked me in like a piece of trash. The parish hall curtains broke my fall. They were old and worn and smelled of smoke. The boys got suspended, but they were only trying to put me in my place. No one likes a puzzle with bits sticking out.

I looked up into the crushed-meringue sky and heard fading laughter, the dumpster boys' and then my parents'. *Fawlty Towers* came to an end and there were footsteps on the stairs. "Wonderwall" faded to black.

CHAPTER TWO

Getting to school on time was pure guesswork because there were no clocks in our house—Dad couldn't stand the ticking. As a clockmaker at Just a Matter of Time, he said his days were filled with a "bloody cacophony of ticks and tocks." He only owned one timepiece, a wristwatch, which he kept in his bedside table and checked just once in the morning, so he could gauge when to leave for work. I left shortly thereafter and hoped for the best.

As always, Uneven Steven greeted me on the corner with a big "'Allo, Squire." I used to correct him by saying "It's Squires, with an *s*," until he told me that calling someone squire in England was the same as saying buddy or fella. It was just one of our many lost-in-translation moments.

We first met on the corner of Cochrane and Duckworth—I was walking past it, he was sprawled across it. I had no problem with the disadvantaged, I was always praying for them at mass, but did they need to take up the whole sidewalk? My foot got caught in his rucksack and I ended up doing a crazy hokeypokey until I was finally freed. I said "arsehole" as I stumbled away. He shouted, "Oi, who you callin' a merry old soul?" I knew nothing about Cockney rhyming slang back then—I just thought he was deaf. The next day as I passed, he gathered his things and said, "Good day, Your Highness. Is the sidewalk to your liking?" I said, "No. You forgot the red carpet." He laughed his head off. It was the beginning of a beautiful friendship.

Uneven Steven spent his mornings on the corner of Cochrane and Duckworth, having spent the night at the Harbour Light Centre. Visiting him required a bit of a detour but I figured school could wait—a top o' the morning to the disadvantaged was far more important.

I returned Steven's *'Allo, Squire* with a "What's the time, me ol' trout?"

Steven looked at his watch. "8:49."

School didn't start till nine. I dropped my schoolbag.

"Loads of time. Congrats on the job, by the way," I said.

"Oh, I don't work at the bingo hall anymore. Frankie McCall fired me after my first shift."

"How come?"

"The Sullivan sisters complained when I called *eighty-eight*."

"What's eighty-eight?"

"Two fat ladies."

"You didn't look at them when you said it, did you?"

"Couldn't help it, mate."

"This'll cheer you up," I said.

I took a homemade roll out of my pocket. "Have a squeeze of me grandmudder's buns."

He took it in his grubby paw and grinned. "Cheeky devil."

I liked giving the disadvantaged a laugh.

"Guess what?" I said. "I'm gonna be a Full Tilt Dancer."

"Irish step dancing?" he said. "If you want to be a dancer, mate, you need to be a bit more rock and roll. I can show you some moves, if you like."

Uneven Steven claimed he was a popular rock star in the sixties and seventies, known for his signature moves. No one believed him. Not when his left leg was three inches shorter than his right.

"I don't like rock and roll," I said. "I like Irish music."

"Ireland is the armpit of Great Britain," said Steven. "And why you'd want to look like a bloody leprechaun dancing around in a tartan vest is beyond me."

I was disgusted. Since when was leprechaun an insult?

"Step dancing," I said through gritted teeth, "is cool."

"Cool? You need your 'ead checked, mate. All that clickin' and clackin'. It's a bloody racket, that's what it is."

I whacked the bun out of his hand like an archer shooting an apple off somebody's head. "What would you know, you stupid limey? You don't know nothing about nothing."

He picked up the roll and flicked off the gravel. "Don't know nothing about nothing?" he said. "That's a double negative, Squire. Double negatives don't make no sense."

For someone who left school at fifteen, Uneven Steven was incredibly smart.

He patted his cardboard square. "'Ave a seat, you silly teapot lid."

Teapot lid. That was a new one.

"Tell me," he said. "Why do you *really* want to join Father O'Flaherty and his poncy dancers?"

I took the dirty roll from him and gave him a new one from my lunch bag. "The thing is," I said, "I need a thing."

"A thing?"

"Pius is a jock. Shelagh's the president of student council. And you," I added to humor him, "you got that whole

BARRY SQUIRES, FULL TILT

rock star thing going. I just want to be part of something."

"And you really want this step dancing malarkey to be your thing?"

"Nanny Squires says I need to do something physical, to get all my angst out."

His blue-gray eyes sparkled through lashes that Shelagh would kill for. "Angst, eh?"

"And I really do think it looks cool. Their feet move so fast and the taps are so loud. It's almost . . . violent. It's like they're kicking the shit out of the floor. The problem is, they audition only once a year—in September."

Uneven Steven took a bite of my grandmother's roll and looked to the sky.

"'Ere's what you do," he said after a minute or two. "Get yourself down to the nursing home and offer to do a performance. Make sure it's a Thursday night, that's when Father O'Flaherty visits. If he sees potential, he might arrange an audition. Better yet, he might invite you to join on the spot."

"A performance?" I said. "In public? I'm good, but I'm no Michael Flatley."

"Don't worry, mate. They're gonna love you."

"My own family laughed their arses off. These old people, they might boo me right off the stage."

"They won't."

"How do you know?"

"There is no stage. According to Alfie Bragg, you stand on an *X* in the Last Chance Saloon."

"The what?"

"The Last Chance Saloon. It's what the residents call the special events lounge."

"Why?"

"Because, mate, it might be the last time they get to see great entertainers such as yourself. They're no spring chickens, you know."

I stood up and put my backpack on. "So no pressure, then."

He swallowed the last bite of bun and patted his stomach. "Ta for this, Squire. It really filled a hole in me old Auntie Nelly."

★

Michael Whelan rushed past me as I made my way toward school. "Better get going, Wine-bar. Bell's gonna go."

I sighed. Mr. McGraw had meant well by telling the class the scientific name for the birthmark across my cheek, but hearing the words "port-wine stain" only gave the bastards more inventive ways to insult me. Wine-bar, a play on my full name, Finbar, quickly caught on. So did Merlot and Cabernet, which were types of wine, not port, so not only were my classmates bastards, they were stupid bastards.

Nanny Squires told me to be confident about my birthmark. She said I was as good as the next person. Better, even. She said, "When you walk into that school you need to act like you own the place." It was good advice. Because when I walked around all cocky and bold, the names bounced off me. But on the bad days, when I woke up wishing I had a different face, I was suddenly an arsehole magnet. It wasn't just "Hey, Merlot," it was "Hey, Barry, you've got a little something on your face," or a chorus of "Freaks Come Out at Night." Damian Clarke and Thomas Budgell were the worst. When we'd moved to junior high, they'd spread the rumor that I was highly contagious and anyone within three feet would be afflicted. They called me Moses for a while after that because of the way I parted the crowd in the hallway like it was the Red Sea. Yep, on the bad days my face was as attention-getting as Frankie McCall's neon sign. It was a beacon for bastards.

I stood outside school for another ten minutes, then went straight to the principal's office.

"Mornin', Judy," I said, slinging my schoolbag around the wooden desk she kept in the corner. "Aren't you a vision of loveliness today? Green is really your color— reminds me of the rolling hills of the Emerald Isle."

"Who sent you here, Barry?" she said. "Whoever it was gave up way too early."

"Well, Judes—"

"That's Mrs. Muckle to you, Mr. Squires."

I smiled. "I think we know each other far too well for silly formaldehydes, don't you?"

"The word you are looking for is *formalities*."

I shrugged. "Ehh, close enough. Starts with an *f*, ends in an *s*."

It was tricky, this balancing act I did each day. The key was to be disruptive enough to be kept out of class, while not being too hard on poor old Judy—it wasn't her fault my face was a beacon for bastards.

"Well?" she said. "Who sent you here?"

"No one. I sent myself."

"Why would you do that?"

"I was extremely late this morning."

She looked at the clock. "For the love of God, Barry, it's not even 9:15. And don't you have English with Mr. McGraw first period? Of all the classes you shouldn't be missing."

I picked up the nameplate on her desk. It was shaped like a Toblerone. "The thing is, Judes, and I'm just being honest with you, I have a feeling if I go to class, I might punch someone in the face. So it's best I stay here."

"What do you mean you *have a feeling*?"

"It's, like, deep down in my bones. I'm feeling a punch coming on—like how Nanny Squires knows when it's going to rain."

"For goodness sake, Barry. Can't you just ignore it?"

"Nanny Squires says I should never deny my feelings. She says us Catholics are repressed enough as it is." I took off my jacket and sat down. "Don't worry. I'll just sit here at my desk and do my work."

"That is not *your* desk."

I wanted to say, *Well, my name's on it,* but thought better of pointing out the *FTS* I'd carved into the wood with the metal pointy thing from my math set.

"I'm practically the only one that uses it. In fact," I said, waving her nameplate through the air, "I could use one of these bad boys myself."

She came around from behind her desk.

"Hiding in here all day won't help," she said.

I stared at her shoes. They were high heels and red. Nan would call them "fantabulous." Mom would call them "slutty."

"You're letting them win, Barry. You deserve to be in the classroom just as much as anyone else. Don't let them drive you away." She looked at me and smiled. "Now get to class."

I looked up. "Judes?"

"Yes?"

"I hope you don't mind me saying, but I like your shoes. They're really fantabulous."

"Mr. Squires?"

"Yeah?"

"If I hear you calling me Judes again, you'll get detention for a week."

I shrugged. "Fair enough."

Thomas Budgell passed me on my way to class. He called me Pinot Noir in an exaggerated French accent. I could have just ignored him, but how could I deny that feeling deep in my bones? It was a short walk back to the principal's office. I said I didn't lay a finger on him but his bloody lip proved otherwise. Thomas was sent back to class but I stayed with Mrs. Muckle. She said, "What am I going to do with you, Barry?" I suggested a game of Go Fish. It was a joke but she took a pack of cards from her desk. "Crazy Eights," she said. "Go Fish drives me cracked."

★

Funny thing happened at gym class that day. Mr. Nolan had us doing the dreaded Canada Fitness Test. We took turns doing flexed-arm hangs, standing long jumps, and sit-ups while Nolan timed, measured, and counted. Only a few people did well at it and I wasn't one of them.

Suddenly, I wasn't Wine-bar. I was "Jesus, Barry, this is hell," and "Christ, Squires, Nolan's going to kill us." For forty minutes, we were all frayed, and I wished hell lasted forever.

★

After school I headed for the nursing home. I passed Uneven Steven on my way.

"How's Judes?" he asked. (He loved my tales from the principal's office.)

"She had a face on her like a smacked arse," I said. "That woman is as crooked as sin."

Steven laughed. "Maybe she'd lighten up if you weren't in so much Barney Rubble all the time."

I passed him what was left of my lunch. "Don't worry," I said. "She'll light up like a Christmas tree when she finds I'm going to perform for the oldies at the nursing home. I'm going there now to set it up."

He unzipped my lunch bag. "Make sure to tell 'em you're good friends with Alfie Bragg," he said, trying to open an Oreo with his sausage-sized fingers. "That way you'll be a shoo-in."

"But I barely know Alfie Bragg."

The Oreo crumbled to bits. "Tell 'em anyway. One little porky pie won't do no harm."

I twisted my last cookie in half and handed it to him. "You're right. Honesty is never the best policy. Remember when I told Judes she'd put on a few over Christmas?"

Steven's grin emerged through his thick beard like the sun coming through a black cloud.

"I tried to warn her," I continued. "I said, 'Judith, my duck, you'd better tell those students you'll only accept non-edible gifts.' But would she listen? No. She kept stuffing her face with Pot of Gold. I knew she'd come back the size of a house."

I waited for Steven to laugh his big, deep *ha-ha-ha*, and when he did, I felt like I'd just scored the winning goal in the biggest sporting event in the world. He slapped his knee and said, "You kill me, Squire, you really kill me." Inside, I was bursting—because laughter is the best medicine and Steven once said he was sick in the head.

"Well, I gotta go," I said. "Cheerio and ta-ta and all that other bullcrap you Brits get on with."

He was still chuckling as I walked away. Not only had I scored the winning goal, I was the MVP.

Heading off to the nursing home meant missing my favorite part of the day—getting Gord up from his nap. Nanny Squires liked him up by 3:30, so I always made sure to be home by 3:20. That way I could spend ten minutes on the floor next to his crib, watching him breathe. Breathing with Gord calmed the army men down. The army men marched through my brain all day long. I didn't know who or what they were fighting but they were angry. They ransacked my thoughts, tossing them aside and breaking them in two. It was hard to explain the army men to Mrs. Muckle or Mr. McGraw. It was easier to let them think I was too lazy to live up to my potential. I loved watching Gord sleep. His little pink lips and rosy-pink cheeks hypnotized me. The army men too. With each fall and rise of the breath, they marched to the barracks and climbed into their cots for a nap.

I'd miss Gord today. Breathing wasn't the same without him.

★

The One Step Closer to God Nursing Home was part hotel, part hospital. Its lobby was impressive, with fancy armchairs and a grand fireplace, but it smelled like Gord's room after a diaper change—strongly deodorized with an underlying scent of bodily functions. Some residents lounged in their Sunday best, others wore pajamas and slippers. One old fella wore a top hat and tails. They all had one thing in common, though: they were ancient. Still, I liked this ragtag group of wrinklies. I mean, who doesn't like old people? They spend their days giving out Werther's and wisdom by the bucketloads, all with a twinkle in their eye. Maybe, I thought, this wasn't about getting noticed by Father O'Flaherty. Maybe, just maybe, this was about giving back. I puffed out my chest and made a beeline for the reception desk. It was time to arrange the performance of a lifetime.

As I crossed the room, a sweet old lady in a bright yellow dress and a flowery sunhat caught my eye. I crouched before her, resting my hands on the armrests of her wheelchair.

"If I may be so bold as to say," I said, gazing into the deep crevices of her old-iferous face, "you are the epiphany of a blooming daffodil on a summer's day."

"It's *epitome*," said the old fella in the top hat and tails. "*Epiphany* is an entirely different animal."

The old lady's voice was a croak. "I wandered lonely as a cloud, that floats on high o'er vales and hills, when all at once I saw a crowd, a host, of golden daffodils."

Wandering? Not with those withered old legs. I wanted to compliment her poem but it wasn't very good, so I said, "I must say, you have the perfect voice for a cartoon witch."

Giving back felt amazing.

I continued on, tipping an imaginary hat to Mr. Top Hat and Tails, who swiftly stuck his cane in my path. I flew into the welcoming arms of an overly made-up woman. "Well, well. Aren't you a handsome young man?" Before I could react, she planted a rather slob-iferous kiss on my cheek. In the spirit of giving, I said, "You're not too bad yourself," but to be honest, she had a face only a mother could love.

I continued on my journey to the reception desk. An old woman in a lavender pantsuit shuffled toward me. Her eyes twinkled like stars. She stopped in front of me. "Why, hello there, sonny."

She opened up a large purse and reached inside. She dug this way and that. Slippery little devils, those Werther's. When her eyes lit up, I put out my hand. A moment later, a crumpled old tissue fluttered toward it. I pulled my hand away in disgust. As I walked onward, I pictured the shiny taps on the bottom of Billy Walsh's shoes. It was the only thing that kept me going.

Finally, I'd arrived. The receptionist smiled. Her name-tag said Patsy, and even though she was old, her hair was dyed purple, like the punks down on Water Street. I was starting to give her the ins and outs of my performance when she said, "We're not fussy, my duck. I'm sure you'll be delightful."

"Shall we say 7 p.m., then?" I said. "Thursday evening?"

"Sure," she said, penciling me in on her empty desk calendar. "Why not?"

I asked if I could see the Last Chance Saloon, and she frowned and said, "If you mean the special events room, it's down the hall and to the left."

There were doors down both sides of the hallway, and in the room behind each one was an old person. I made sure to give each and every one of them a nod and a wink because Nan always told me not to tar people with the same brush and just because three wrinklies tried to kill me—one with a cane, one with a kiss, and one with a germ-filled snot-rag—I shouldn't assume they were all a bunch of bastards. My open-mindedness paid off when a little old lady looked up from a book and winked back. I popped my head in her door. "How ya doin' today, missus?"

She said, "Not too bad, considering."

"Considering what?"

She threw her hands up in the air. I took that to mean everything.

"What's your name?" I asked.

"Edie."

"Don't let the bastards get you down, Edie."

She smiled. Good ol' Nan—her words of wisdom were quickly becoming the most useful phrase in my whole vocabulary.

"I'm Barry Squires," I said.

She cocked her head like a dog hearing the word *walk*.

"Aren't you the youngster who punched a hole through the confessional screen?"

"The one and only." I grinned.

The guy came over with some Windex and a cloth. "You shouldn't joke about things like that."

"It wasn't a joke," I said. "It was a lie."

I pointed at the Windex. "When that bottle's empty can you save it for me?"

He shrugged. "Sure. Why?"

"I'm gonna bottle and sell me some St. John's Mist."

"You're going to sell it to yourself?" he said. "That's a terrible business plan."

"Don't be obtuse," I said.

He snorted. "Like you know what that means."

"Annoyingly insensitive or slow to understand," I said. "It's what my English teacher called me when I asked him how Shake's pear could have possibly written *Romeo and Juliet*. A piece of fruit can't write a book. It doesn't even have hands. When he called me obtuse, I thought he was calling me fat but that's *obese*. If it wasn't for the dictionary, I'd have probably got him fired."

Windex guy laughed. "You're funny, kid."

"I called my brother *fermented* once. What I actually meant was *de*-mented. *Fer*-mented means slowly turning into alcohol. Although he did smell like beer once. After a school dance. He threatened to punch my lights out if I told Mom and Dad. I like words. If only they weren't so easily confused."

The guy put down his cleaning supplies and stuck out his hand. "I'm Tony."

I ignored his hand and sang, "Tony Chestnut Knows I Love You." I pointed to all the right body parts at all the right times: toe, knee, chest, head, nose, eyes, and heart. I ended with a big double-point at Tony.

"You're weird, kid."

"I sing that one to Gord all the time."

I looked out the window.

"God almighty!"

I ran outside to find Gord rolling down Duckworth.

"Somebody catch that baby!"

I caught him just as he rolled onto Prescott.

I said, "Don't cry, Gord," but he wasn't crying—he was laughing his sweet baby belly laugh.

I laughed too. "You're cracked, Gord."

We continued on, passing a tourist shop full of T-shirts and souvenirs. I pictured St. John's Mist in the front window. It could be a bestseller.

Down at the harbor there was a cruise ship as tall as Atlantic Place. It had been in Ireland and Florida and New York. I hoped they weren't expecting spring weather. I could almost see my breath today. Gord and I smiled as the passengers filed off. "Go to Caines if you want a real Newfoundland experience," I told them. "Boo makes a mean Jiggs Dinner."

An older woman in a yellow leisure suit stopped. "What's a Jiggs Dinner?" she asked.

"Salt beef, cabbage, potatoes, turnip, and carrots," I said. "All boiled together into a delicious concoction of salty goodness."

She smiled at her husband. "These Newfies sure are friendly."

Nan hated the word Newfie. She said it was a slur. Mom, on the other hand, didn't mind it at all. I was about to tell the woman to be careful, that using the term could cause offense, when her husband passed me a five-dollar bill. "Here ya go, champ." I tucked the money into my pocket. Five dollars' worth of candy at Caines was worth way more than giving a lesson on social justice. I gave the husband a wink. "Thanks, skipper."

Next to the cruise ship was a navy ship offering tours. The sign said ALL CHILDREN MUST BE ACCOMPANIED BY AN ADULT, so Gord and I quickly slipped on behind a blue-eyed family of four. We were heading up the gangplank when another kid tagged along behind us. I gave his brown skin a once-over. "Take a hike. You're going to blow our cover."

"Frig off, b'y," he said. "I'll do what I likes, how I likes, whenever I likes it."

His Newfoundland accent was thicker than mine. "Sorry. I thought—"

"I knows what ya thought," he said. "It's called stereo-typing. Give me a cut of that money you fleeced off that tourist and we'll forget all about it."

I liked this kid. He was a sly one. A real sleveen. Like me.

"How about we go to Caines after the tour?" I said. "I'll buy you a bag of roast chicken chips."

"Throw in a bottle of birch beer and you've got a deal."

I gave him a wink. "Done."

The blond family was moving to the upper deck. "Come on," he said. "Mom and Dad will wonder where we're to."

I laughed. "Like anyone's gonna believe you belong to them."

"Whatever," he said. "If we gets kicked off, we gets kicked off. There's plenty of other no good to get up to today."

I grinned. "I'm Finbar. You can call me Barry."

"Saibal," he said. "Saibal Sharma."

"Sigh-bull," I repeated. "Bulls don't sigh."

"That's because they're too busy running around china shops," he said.

"Ha!" I said. "Good one."

I tried to pull Gord out of his stroller. "Come on, fatso." Saibal helped.

We sang the Village People's "In the Navy" as we climbed the stairs to the upper deck. We were met with disapproving frowns.

A navy man glared at us. "Could you keep it down? I'm *trying* to give a presentation here."

I gave him a jaunty salute. "Aye, aye, captain."

The presentation was boring. Saibal rolled his eyes. I pretended to yawn. The navy man asked if there were any questions. I raised my hand.

"What's long and hard and full of seamen?"

Except for Saibal's snort beside me, the deck fell silent.

"That's very inappropriate," said the navy man.

"Inappropriate how?" asked Saibal. "The answer's 'a submarine.'"

I spoke to Gord in a baby voice. "Some people have the dirtiest minds, don't they?"

The navy man growled. "Where are your parents?"

I looked at the family nearby. The father looked away. "Dad," I said. "How could you?"

The navy man moved toward us.

"Run!" said Saibal.

We took off down the stairs. Saibal snatched the stroller for a quick getaway. When we got out of sight, he set it back down.

"You, sir," I said, "are a scholar and a gentleman."

Saibal looked impressed.

We settled Gord into his seat and headed down Water Street.

At the war memorial, Saibal paused. "Hang on."

He approached a couple of tourists and spoke in a singsong-y accent. "Can you spare some change for a poor refugee? I am so verrry, verrry hungry."

He came back with a handful of coins.

"Geez, b'y," I said. "If you rolled your *r*'s any harder, you'd break your tongue."

"Nah," he said. "My mother tongue is so thick, you'd need a sledgehammer to break it."

At Caines, Boo thanked me for sending tourists his way and gave us 20 percent off. Saibal used his change to buy a bowl of turkey soup, and when we got outside he gave it to a woman begging on the corner.

We sat on the cold, brown grass near the war memorial. Saibal held Gord in his lap.

"You know," I said, opening my birch beer, "you were kind of stereotyping *yourself* with those tourists."

"Hey," he said, "if people are going to assume I'm a refugee, I might as well work it to my advantage."

"People around here wouldn't assume that," I said.

He gave Gord a lick of his chip. "*You* did."

"No, I didn't."

"Yes, you did. When you told me to take a hike, you

made a walking gesture with your fingers because you figured I didn't speak English."

"I did?"

He popped the Gord-licked chip into his mouth. "Yep."

"Oh. Sorry about that. But, for the most part, I think Newfoundlanders are pretty open to people of different races."

"Do me a favor, Finbar," he said. "Don't act like you know what it's like to be brown in this town, because you don't."

"Ha! Brown in this town. That rhymes."

Saibal grinned. "Yeah. I'm a poet and didn't even comprehend that that was the case."

I laughed. "You can call me Barry, by the way."

"I think I'll stick with Finbar," he said.

"Why?"

He drained the last of his birch beer. "Because only a Finbar would call me a scholar and a gentleman. A Barry could never be so distinguished."

"Righty-ho," I said, standing up and dusting myself off. "Finbar it is."

I put Gord back in his stroller and tipped an imaginary hat to Saibal. "Now I must bid you good day. See you tomorrow?"

He smiled. "I'll be here."

CHAPTER FOUR

Back at home, I watched *Riverdance* for ten minutes. I didn't feel the need to watch any more. After all, I had the technical side of Irish step dancing down pat. What I needed to work on was balance and light-footedness. Mom said if I broke one more of her grandmother's tea-cups, she'd nail my feet to the floor. I said, "You'd crucify me over a broken cup?" and she said, "Those cups are bone china, you know."

I decided that in order to dance with lightness and grace, I'd need to dress the part. I went to Nan's closet. It was full of possibilities. (And lacy garments I'd never unsee.) I tried on a white blouse with frilly sleeves. In a move that could only be described as bold, I left the bottom few buttons undone so that I could tie the ends together just above my belly button. A button fell off, but that was okay. Nan said being an artiste was about breaking boundaries and I was awesome at breaking things.

Michael Flatley would never wear polyester slacks from Kmart, so I moved from Nan's closet to my sister's, where I borrowed on a permanent basis a pair of her black leggings. For the first time in my life I was jealous of the female sex. They could keep their periods and maxi-pads and cramps and bras . . . but leggings? They were like a second skin. I knew without a doubt that these super-stretchy wonder pants were going to make my wildest dreams possible. I, Finbar T. Squires, was going to end my routine with the splittiest splits in the history of dance.

It was time to put the training program I'd dreamt up the night before into action. It was really quite good. Groundbreaking, even. Someday I'd make an instructional video for other dancers. I mean, why keep such a secret weapon to myself? But sharing my untested-but-sure-to-be-brilliant idea with the masses would have to wait—I had the performance of a lifetime to prepare for.

I went to the basement and put on the footwear that would revolutionize the dance world.

Hockey skates.

I walked around and around in circles.

The blades made a satisfying click on the concrete floor.

I was a bit wobbly at first but by the tenth lap I was feeling incredibly stable. It was as if I was wearing a pair of Nan's orthopedic shoes. I stood on one foot for forty-five seconds, then switched to the other. Incredibly, both my core and butt muscles were engaged.

This was SO going to work as a training program for dancers. I mean, everyone could get their hands on a pair of skates, and now I could claim proven results in only five minutes!

If only my training program had a name.

I walked around in circles and thought some more.

I needed something catchy. Something fierce.

Then it hit me.

The Balance and Stability Training Academy 4 Real Dancers.

BASTARD for short.

I decided it was time for a dress rehearsal. I mean, why hide my talent away in a basement?

I floated up the stairs with Shelagh's portable CD player in tow and went out to the road where there were no china cabinets to shake or teacups to break. I was feeling pretty positive. If I could Irish step dance in hockey skates, just imagine what I could do in the tap shoes I was planning to borrow on a permanent basis from Billy Walsh!

Little Len from next door came outside and watched as I set up in the middle of the road. I gave him a wink. "Enjoy the show."

I pressed Play, not really caring what came on (I could dance to anything), and got into my opening position (the matador one). When Michael Jackson's "Thriller" blasted through the speakers, I moon-skated from the Coadys' front door to the Merchants'. The blades screeched against the pavement like nails on a chalkboard. I told Little Len to turn up the music. Neighbors emerged from their front doors. I pinned my arms to my sides and broke out into a mighty fine step dance. As a nod to the King of Pop, I interspersed the Irishness of my performance with a few crotch grabs and pelvic thrusts. I grabbed the sky and when I brought it to my heart, I saw faces filling the second-floor windows, and by God those faces were smiling. Not only was I breaking barriers in the dance world, I was single-handedly bringing happiness to the people of York Street.

It was time for my big finish.

I waited for the music to end.

Then—

R-i-i-i-i-p.

The splittiest splits really were the splittiest.

A cold blast of air wafted through the arse of my wonder pants.

I quickly sat on my knees and smiled at God.

In the silence that followed, I heard a scream.

"Get my bloody skates off your bloody feet!"

I turned around. As Pius got closer, his anger turned to horror. "What the hell are you wearing?"

I rolled onto my arse and tried to bum-scootch away, but Pius pulled me along by the blades.

"Pius! Stop! I'm getting road burn!"

He dragged me to the sidewalk and roughly tugged off the skates.

"Good God, Barry. You're such an embarrassment."

I followed him, stocking-footed, toward the house. Nan and Gord were in the doorway. Nan started to clap. Good ol' Nan. One person clapping was always followed by another, then another . . . that's how it worked. I looked around. The neighbors just stood there like a bunch of bastards.

When Nan's applause trailed off, I bowed, because the number one rule in the entertainment biz is never let them see you sweat. On the outside I was as cool as a cucumber, but on the inside I felt a growling, deep inside my belly. I gave a final wink and a wave before stepping into the house, where I immediately swung for Pius. He caught my arm. "Calm down, Fin-bear."

"You ruined my performance," I growled.

"You dulled my blades," he said.

"I was *trying* to making my dream a reality."

He let go of my arm with a shove. "How is dressing like a pirate and dancing on hockey skates a dream?"

"I was practicing," I said. "Success doesn't come overnight, you know."

"You'll never be a dancer, Barry," he said. "You've got terrible rhythm and no pizzazz."

"How dare you?" I yelled.

"Baaaaa-daaaaa!" yelled Gord.

"Shhh," said Nan, bouncing Gord in her arms. "Your mother's resting."

Shelagh walked in with an armful of books. "Are those my leggings?"

I shook my head. "No."

She looked closer. "They are. I can't believe you're wearing my leggings."

"I don't know what you're talking about," I said.

She gestured to my crotch. "Ew. Gross. Your *thing* is stretching the material."

I looked down. My crotchticular region *was* looking rather pronounced. I smiled. "Thanks, Shelagh."

"You should see the back of them," said Pius. "He's torn the arse right out of them."

"Mom! Barry wrecked my leggings!"

"Shhh," said Nan.

"And he's wearing Nan's shirt!" Pius called.

"For the love of God," said Nan. "Keep it down."

But we didn't want to keep it down.

"Aaaaaaaaaaah!" I shouted.

We looked to the ceiling. A moment later, a bed squeak. We waited for a "Jesus, Mary, and Joseph, will ye give it a rest," but all we heard was silence.

Shelagh and Pius looked to the floor.

I cleared my throat and hooked my thumbs into my waistband.

Shelagh looked up. "What are you doing?"

"You wanted your pants back, didn't you?"

"Oh, for God's sake," said Nan.

I wiggled my hips from side to side. Shelagh covered her eyes. "Please don't."

I slid the leggings down to my ankles.

Pius grinned. "You're cracked, Barry."

I slipped one foot out, then the other.

"Here you go," I said, holding them out for Shelagh. "You wanted them. Take them."

When she uncovered her eyes, I swung them through the air like a lasso. I gyrated my hips with each spin.

"Ew, Barry," she screamed. "Stop that!"

"Oh my God," said Pius. "He's got a hole in his undies."

They were laughing but that was the point. If making them smile involved a sneak peek at my genitalia, then so be it.

I spun the leggings two, three, four more times and then let them go. They flew through the air and landed on Shelagh's head. We laughed loudly; Gord too. I wondered if Mom was listening upstairs. I hoped she was. I hoped she knew what she was missing.

★

Takeout meant Mom didn't feel like cooking, and when Mom didn't feel like cooking, Nan and Dad usually didn't bother either—they just threw their hands up in the air as if to say, "What's the point?" As for the rest of us, well, we wouldn't know how to cook if our lives depended on it—which they kind of did, really. I mean, if you didn't eat, you'd die. Maybe that was what Mom wanted. To die. After all, she barely ate. All she'd had for breakfast that morning was three single Cheerios. She'd picked them off Gord's chin when I brought him to her for a cuddle. I was thrilled when I saw how he made her smile but on reflection it was no big deal. I mean, you'd have to be the Wicked Witch of the West not to smile at Gord.

I sat in the front window watching neighbors coming and going. There was condensation on the glass. I drew a penis. There was a doily on a side table next to me. I put it on my head. Our car puttered up and pulled over. I let the window sheers drop and waited. A moment later

Dad came in. He had six cold plates from Caines. "What do you have on your head, you fool?" I pulled off the doily and he ruffled my hair. We sat at the table, all six of us. Mom's supper was in the fridge. When I was done eating, I brought it up to her. I sat at the foot of her bed and watched her nibble the turkey, pick at the potato salad, and lick a beet. She seemed interested in my description of Mrs. Muckle's fantabulous shoes, and when I told her the rumor about old Judes having an affair with Roger Graham from Graham's Groceries, her eyebrows went up. I hadn't seen Mom's eyebrows go up in a long time, so I told her that Mrs. Muckle and Roger Graham were caught having an intimate moment in the walk-in freezer at Graham's Groceries. It wasn't true but Mom smiled in disgust, so I kept going. "Mrs. Graham caught them," I said. "Mrs. Muckle claimed that Mr. Graham was just warming her up, but Mrs. Graham said she wasn't born yesterday and slammed the door on them. The next morning a cashier found them and called 911. It took them three days to thaw out." Mom's eyebrows went up again, this time in doubt. I'd gone too far. "How about these cold plates?" I said. "Pretty good, huh?"

"They're okay," she said, pushing aside the savory dressing.

"Boo makes that himself, you know," I said. "He calls it *stuffing*, for the Americans who come off the cruise ships. Even *they* think it's the best part of the cold plate."

"It's delicious," said Mom. "I'm just not that hungry right now."

"Guess what?" I said, thinking up another lie. "At school we went on a field trip to Mount Scio Farm, where savory is made."

"Is that right?" said Mom.

"Yep. The owner said savory has many health benefits. It helps with sore muscles, concentration, energy, and mood."

I raised my eyebrows when I said *mood*.

Mom stared at her dinner with wet eyes.

I reached for the plate. "I'll take this downstairs."

"Leave it," she said.

I looked at the flowers on her nightgown. They were forget-me-nots, the kind Dad wore on his lapel on Memorial Day. I chewed the skin around my thumbnail. Mom reached out, lowered my hand.

"Tell me more about Mrs. Muckle and Roger Graham," she said.

I let out the breath I didn't know I'd been holding.

"Well," I said, "apparently Mrs. Muckle had frostbite on her nipples."

Mom scooped up some dressing and smiled.

★

Later that evening, I sat on Gord's floor and sang him a bedtime song. I made a different one up each night. Tonight's was called "The Lovely Lass with the Gargantuan Ass." It was about a girl who let her siblings use her butt as a pillow. My favorite line was "The sea of children suddenly parted when the lovely lass unexpectedly farted."

Coincidentally, later in bed, Pius let one rip.

I said, "Remind me to never use your butt as a pillow."

He stuck his nose further into his book. "Shut up, weirdo."

I closed my eyes, then opened them again.

"Pius? Do you think Mom—"

"I said shut up."

He put his book down and turned off the light.

I closed my eyes once again and drifted off to dreamland, where Saibal and I shared a birch beer in India.

★

The next morning, I had a few minutes to spare, so I plunked down on Uneven Steven's piece of cardboard and told him every detail of my performance on York Street the day before.

"You wore a frilly top and your sister's leggings?" he said.

"Yep. But, to be honest, I'm not sure I'm cut out for this dancing malarkey. My brother says I have no pizzazz. Maybe I should just drop the whole thing."

"Don't be daft," said Steven. "Do you think I would have played with the Beatles in '64 if I had given up on my dream?"

I smiled. "You played with the Beatles? Wow. That's impressive."

"Don't listen to the naysayers, Squire. I believe in you."

I gathered my things and stood up. "So you'll come to the performance at the nursing home?"

Steven grinned. "I wouldn't miss it."

★

I went straight to the office and pointed at the clock.

"Look! It's 9:05."

Mrs. Muckle reached under her desk and pulled out a bag.

"For you."

I looked inside. "An alarm clock?"

She nodded. "Mr. McGraw got it down at the Sally Ann."

I was both touched and horrified.

I gestured to the chair across from her. "May I?"

She poured herself a cup of tea. "Two minutes."

I took a seat. "I have a new friend," I said. "He's a refugee. From India."

Mrs. Muckle looked intrigued. "Really?"

"I met him downtown. I bought him some birch beer because his lips were dry. I don't think he'd had a drop to drink in days."

She raised an eyebrow.

"Come to think of it," I said, smacking my lips together, "I'm feeling a tad parched myself."

She poured some tea into a second mug. "You're only getting half a cup."

I shook my head. "If we all had your attitude, Judes, refugees would be dying of thirst all over the place."

She set the pot down. "Don't call me Judes."

I took a slurp of my tea. "Guess what?"

"What?"

"If I fail eighth grade, we'll get to spend another year together."

"You're not going to fail eighth grade, Barry."

"I might."

"You won't. Your grades are just about good enough. Thanks be to Jesus."

"But if I did, it'd be okay, right? I mean, another year might do me good."

"Barry, I know going to a new school is scary—"

"I'm not scared."

I took another slurp of my tea.

"Guess what else?" I said, changing the subject.

Mrs. Muckle sighed. "What?"

"Gord can sit up for six seconds without falling on his face."

Her face lit up. "Is that right?"

I beamed with pride. "He's pretty advanced for his age."

"And how's your mother?" she asked.

Dad had been in to talk to Mrs. Muckle about "the situation" and now she was nosier than ever. Caring, almost.

"She's like a yo-yo," I said.

"Up and down?" said Mrs. Muckle.

I nodded. "She didn't even eat the dressing on her cold plate last night. I mean, where would we be if we all refused savory when we felt a little down? It's our duty as Newfoundlanders to eat it. I mean, if Mount Scio Farm goes out of business, we're doomed. We might as well kiss goodbye all that makes us stand out as a unique culture."

"Don't be so foolish," said Mrs. Muckle. "Mount Scio Farm will never go out of business. Savory is like crack around here."

"If it was like crack," I said, "Mom would have wolfed down her supper like there was no tomorrow. But maybe she doesn't care about tomorrows—maybe she just cares about herself, and that's why she stays in her room all day and leaves the rest of us wandering around wondering if she'll ever come out."

Mrs. Muckle reached for me. "Barry—"

I pulled my hand away. "Thanks a bunch, Judes. Your prying has made me late for class. And on the one day I show up early too."

She looked at the clock. "I suppose 9:05 *is* early by your standards."

I drained my tea and made a face. "Where did ya get your teabags? The bottom of St. John's Harbour? You'd think on a principal's salary you could get some bags made with quality leaves. What are ya? From the mainland or something? Geez."

She sighed. "That's enough, Barry."

"Is it?" I said. "I'm not so sure. I could go on about this for days. Because that tea tastes like crap. Like actual crap. Like a cup of warmed-up shit."

Mrs. Muckle stood up. "Get out, Barry."

"My pleasure," I said.

I wasn't lying. It *was* a pleasure. Things were back to normal. I was the annoyer and she was the annoyee. Anything more than that involved feelings, and the last thing I wanted to feel was feelings.

I stood in front of Mr. McGraw's door and took a deep breath. A moment later I waltzed in like I owned the place.

"Top o' the morning, Mr. McGraw. How's it hanging?"

"You're late, Finbar. You need to get a late slip from Mrs. Muckle."

"Mrs. Muckle?" I said. "That old windbag is the reason I'm late. She invited me for tea in her office and spent a good twenty minutes talking about the quality of her bags."

Mr. McGraw looked skeptical. I nodded to the phone on the wall. "Call her if you want."

He shook his head. "Just sit down and get to work."

I paused before heading to my desk. "Might I ask, sir, does our little 'incentive' deal still apply even though I'm a tad late?"

He looked at the clock and nodded. There was still forty minutes left and I was in the mood for saltwater taffy. If I made it to the end of class, I'd pick a blue one.

I took my seat. We'd been working on our persuasive essays. Mine was blank except for the stick man I'd drawn in the margins. His name was Twig.

I gave Twig a hat.

Everyone around me was writing furiously.

I wondered what I could write about.

I gave a Twig a penis and laughed out loud. Mr. McGraw gave me a warning look.

I gave Twig a pair of tartan pants.

And a vest.

Good old Twig. He was an inspiration.

I wrote my title: *Why I Should Be Given One Hundred and Twenty-Five Dollars for a Tartan Outfit and Tap Shoes.*

I looked to the ceiling and thought about what being a Full Tilt Dancer would mean to me. I started with "Dancing is my life" and thought some more.

I stared at the back of Karen Crocker's head. Her braids were uneven. I tapped her on the shoulder. "Who did your hair this morning? Your one-eyed nan or your drunk mother?"

Her hand shot up in the air. "Sir, Barry thinks he's funny but he's not."

Mr. McGraw's warning look got warn-ier.

Damian Clarke was in the desk across from me. He leaned over. "Guess what? My essay is almost done. It's called 'Why Everyone in St. John's Should Chip In and Get Barry Squires Some Plastic Surgery for That Thing on His Face.'"

Normally I'd have punched him in the nose but there was the saltwater taffy to think of—not to mention Mr. McGraw's undying faith in me.

I raised my hand. "Sir? Would you happen to have a thesaurus? I'm writing my essay on 'Why I Hate Damian Clarke,' but I'm overusing the word *arsehole.*"

Mr. McGraw frowned. "Mind your mouth, Finbar."

"I'm sorry," I said, "but I'm running out of descripa-tory words. I mean, I've used *dickhead* ten times already, and I've positively exhausted the word *fuckface*."

Mr. McGraw walked toward me in a rage.

I put my hands up. "Whoa there, Trigger—"

He grabbed me by the elbow. "Out."

"Geez," I said. "You really don't want me to have that saltwater taffy, do you?"

He pulled me out of the classroom and into the hall-way. He put his face in mine and said, "Don't act like I'm the one breaking the deal here. You know exactly what you're doing."

Something inside me shook. It felt like my heart but it was probably my soul.

"Well?" he said. "What are you waiting for? You've got what you wanted. You're free to go. Have fun hiding in Mrs. Muckle's office all day."

I tried to think of something to say that would make his face go from red to its normal pasty white.

"Tomorrow will be different," I said. "I'm going to write the best, most heartfelt essay you've ever read. It'll be enough to bring a tear to a glass eye."

His rolled his eyes.

"Watch yourself," I said. "Remember what I said about Thomas Budgell's father's sister's daughter."

He didn't laugh.

"Just go, Barry," he said. "I've got a class full of students waiting to learn. I've spent enough time on you."

For some reason my feet wouldn't move.

McGraw waved me away. "Go."

"Sir, I . . ."

What I wanted to say was stuck in my throat. "Damian, he . . ." I put my hand to my cheek. It was such a small part of me—why was it the whole to everyone else?

"Finbar," said Mr. McGraw. "You can't control what other people say, but you can control how you react to them."

Billy Walsh appeared in the hallway. When he saw us, he step danced his way to the bathroom. Mr. McGraw applauded. It didn't surprise me. The Full Tilt Dancers were gods in this school.

"Maybe," I said, "step dancing could be the whole of me."

Mr. McGraw looked puzzled. "What?"

"Nothing."

I felt his eyes on me as I walked away.

As I turned the corner, I saw him fiddling with something in his pocket.

I wasn't too fond of saltwater taffy anyway.

★

Damian passed me in the hallway. "Look who it is! Chardonnay!"

I could've just told him that chardonnay was actually a white wine. That would've been enough to shut him up. But I punched him in the nose instead. The gym teacher heard the ruckus and dragged us to the office by the scruff of our necks.

Mrs. Muckle gave Damian a wad of tissues for his nose and sent him to the nurse.

She gave me a look of despair and told me to write an apology.

I settled into my desk. "I'll do my very best to make this genuine," I promised. "No matter how long it takes."

Then I began:

Dear Damian,

I'm sorry you are an arshole . . .

Mrs. Muckle looked over my shoulder. "Your *arsehole* is missing an *e*."

"An *e*?" I said. "That would make it *earshole*. Damian's full of shit, not wax."

She pointed to the door. "Out. You know how I feel about swearing."

"Actually," I said, "I *don't* know how you feel about swearing. I mean, how is *shit* worse than *arsehole*? And where does the f-word fit in? Maybe you could make me an easy-to-follow flowchart. I'd like to know where you stand on all this."

She walked to the door and opened it. "Go."

Poor woman, she was completely frazzled. I stood outside her office and gave her a moment to compose herself. When I returned thirty seconds later, she looked like a deer caught in the headlights.

"Oh, Judes," I said. "Don't you know you can't fill the emptiness inside you with food?"

She shouted "out!" again. A piece of Twix flew from her mouth. It landed by my foot. I wasn't sure what to do. Leaving it there seemed wrong. Especially when there were children starving in Africa. I picked it up and offered it to her. "Did you want this or . . ."

Her face turned the color of her fantabulous slut shoes.

I gave her a wide berth as I walked to the garbage bin under her desk. I paused behind her.

"I hope you don't mind me saying," I said, "but you seem a bit on edge. Perhaps you shouldn't be alone right now. I'll stay if you like. Just for one more period. Even though I'd hate to miss math."

"You can stay," she sighed. "But if I hear another word out of you . . ."

I dropped the Twix chunk in the garbage and backed away with my hands up. "You won't even know I'm here."

I sat down and rubbed my hands together over the apology letter. "Now," I said. "Time to return to the task I'd been working on so enthusiastically before you interrupted me with your nitpicky criticism."

She sucked in her breath.

I turned to her. "You know, you need to be more mindful of your breathing," I said. "Especially if you want to find inner peace." I stuck my fingers in my ears. "Watch and learn."

I inhaled through my nose, then exhaled through my mouth. *Bzzzzzzz.*

"Bumblebee breathing," I said. "I learned it at an anger management class my mother forced me to go to. It relieves stress, especially the angry kind. Apparently it takes a lot of practice. It hasn't worked for me yet. Which is not surprising. I'm not good at anything."

She threw me the other half of her Twix. "You're good at driving me nuts, I can tell ya that."

I wasn't sure that was the most appropriate thing for a school official to say to a student, but I gave her a wink and took a bite of the bar. "You're the bee's knees, Judes."

CHAPTER FIVE

After school I bundled Gord up and went to the war memorial. Saibal was already there with two birch beers and a giant sour key for Gord.

"He can't have that," I said. "He has no teeth."

Saibal put his pointer finger through the hole in the top and popped the long end in Gord's mouth.

"You don't need teeth to suck," he said. "And don't worry, I'll hold it so he doesn't choke."

Gord made a sour face on the first lick.

"He doesn't like it," I said.

A second later he was leaning forward with his tongue out, gagging for more.

"He loves it," said Saibal, popping it back in. "Just make sure you rinse his mouth out after so he doesn't get cavities."

"Even though he has no teeth?" I said, opening my can of pop. "Duly noted."

Saibal looked impressed. "You really have a way with words, Finbar."

"I have to admit," I said, "for the longest time I thought it was *Julie noted*. Then I saw it written down."

"Imagine if your name was Julie," he said. "Instead of saying okay, you could say 'Julie noted.'"

"Julie, dear, don't forget you have a dentist appointment at three," I said.

"Julie noted," said Saibal in a female voice.

I laughed and pointed to my face. "This is a port-wine stain, by the way."

Saibal wiped some drool off Gord's chin. "So?"

"I just thought you might be wondering."

"Why would I?"

I shrugged. "I dunno."

He crushed his empty can with his one hand. "So. What no good should we get up to today?"

"I want to buy a *Playboy* magazine."

"Ew," said Saibal.

"Not for me," I said. "For Billy Walsh. I need to borrow

his tap shoes. I figure a naked lady magazine would be a good trade."

"What makes you think he'd want a *Playboy* magazine?"

"He looks like a bit of a pervert."

Saibal shrugged. "Fair enough."

I puffed out my chest. "Guess what? I'm going to be a Full Tilt Dancer."

"Really?" said Saibal. "I tried out last year but Father Molloy said I wasn't a good fit."

He put finger quotes around the word *fit*.

"What are you suggesting?" I said.

"I'm suggesting I didn't have the right look."

He didn't put quotes around the word *look*, but I caught his drift.

"Father Molloy may be a fedora-wearing thieving jerk," I said, "but he's no racist."

Saibal frowned. "How do you know?"

"I just do."

"How?"

"Because Newfoundlanders aren't like that."

"Do tell," said Saibal, popping the sour key from Gord's mouth to his own.

"Way back in history," I said, "there was a black man from the US who ended up on a beach in Newfoundland after a shipwreck. People saved him and nursed him back to good health and he was amazed because back at home, white people weren't nice to him. In Newfoundland, he was treated like all the other survivors."

Saibal threw the soggy sour key in the grass. "Nice story. Now tell me, how does that prove Father Molloy can't be racist?"

"It doesn't."

"Exactly."

"I'm just saying—"

"Don't be so naive, Finbar. Open your eyes and look around."

I did.

"Get a room!" I shouted to a couple making out under a tree.

Saibal laughed. "Come on," he said. "Time to buy some porn."

We headed toward Water Street.

The panhandlers knew Saibal by name.

"How come I've never seen you around here before?" I asked.

"I live in King William Estates," he said. "I wasn't allowed to get the bus until I turned twelve."

"King William Estates, huh? You must be loaded."

"My dad's a family doctor and my mom's a cardiologist."

"Does she use those big paddles like they do on TV?"

Saibal jumped in front of me and hit my chest with an imaginary defibrillator. "Clear!"

I jolted with an almighty shock.

"What do *your* parents do?" asked Saibal.

"Nothing as good as yours," I said. "Mom was a lunch lady before Gord was born and Dad fixes clocks."

"Interesting," said Saibal, even though it wasn't.

When we got to Atlantic Place, Saibal helped me carry the stroller up the steps.

The top shelf of the magazine shop had lots of choices.

"What do you think, Saibal?" I said. "They have *Penthouse* and *Hustler* too."

"Get the *Playboy*," he said. "Then, when you give it to Billy Walsh, you can say, 'A *Playboy* for a playboy.'"

I grinned. "I like the way you think, Saibal."

The lady behind the counter wouldn't sell us the magazine, so I gave it to Gord. When he ripped the cover in half, Saibal pointed to the YOU BREAK IT, YOU BUY IT sign. He slapped a five-dollar bill on the counter. "That should cover it."

We left before she could protest.

Back on Water Street, Saibal said, "When you think about it, my mom and your dad do the same thing. They both get things ticking again."

I liked that Saibal thought my dad and his mom were the same. I pictured my dad standing over a timepiece shouting, "Clear!"

"What are you smiling about?" said Saibal.

"Nothing," I said. "Come on. It's time to trade some porn for a dream."

★

The dancers practiced at the Benevolent Irish Society, or BIS as we called it. I caught Billy Walsh's eye from the window. A moment later, he was outside.

"What do you want, Squires?"

I gave him a devilish grin.

"A *Playboy*," I said, "for a playboy."

He looked confused. "What?"

Saibal elbowed me in the ribs. "Finbar. The magazine."

I looked around. "Gord! You dirty thing!"

His face was right in the centerfold.

I gave the magazine to Billy and proposed the deal. His eyes widened as he scanned the pages. He took his shoes off right then and there.

"I want them back in good condition."

I told him he could keep the magazine.

We went back to York Street to drop the shoes off.

When I got to the doorstep, Nan looked beyond me into the street.

"Who's that?" she said.

"That's Saibal," I said. "He's my—"

"Why is he on the curb?" she said. "Is he begging?"

"No, he—"

"He's begging, isn't he? Poor little thing. These refugees, they have a hard time when they first arrive, God love 'em."

"Nan. He's not—"

"Come over, my ducky," she yelled. "Come in and I gives ya some supper."

Saibal walked over and took Nan's hand in both of his. "Thank you so verrry, verrry much. I am so verrry, verrry hungry."

Nan was charmed. "God love his cotton socks."

I elbowed him in the side. "Drop the act, will ya? It's annoying."

He smiled. "I'm just filling the role that is expected of me," he whispered.

"Come in, come in," said Nan. "I'm just about to put supper on the table."

It was a home-cooked meal for once and I was glad. Mom's empty chair was a lot less depressing when we weren't eating off paper plates.

There was also a rack of freshly baked tea buns cooling in the kitchen. Saibal reached for one. "May I?"

I'd have had my hand smacked this close to supper but Nan smiled and said, "Yes, my duck. Take as many as you want."

Pius strutted in and nodded toward Saibal. "Who's that?"

"A refugee," whispered Nan. "Starved to death, the poor thing."

Pius passed him another bun.

When Dad and Shelagh came in, it was the same. One whisper from Nan and they were filled with compassion.

"I should call home," said Saibal, his accent thick. "Hopefully my mother can make it to the phone. Her legs, they do not work so well anymore. And my father, well, he is probably out begging."

I ignored the collective "awww" from my family and pulled Saibal roughly into the living room. "How long are you planning on keeping this up?"

He patted his stomach. "Until my tummy is verrry, verrry full."

His fake accent was getting on my last nerve.

He picked up the phone and called home. "What are ya at, Mudder? Me? I'm fine. Best kind. Listen, I got invited to a friend's house for supper. Yup . . . yup . . . yup. Okay, Mudder. Loves ya."

He hung up. "I have to get the seven-thirty bus back to King William," he said. "I hope I have time for dessert. If your nan's tea buns are anything to go by, dessert's gonna be tasty."

We turned toward the kitchen to find Pius standing at the door with his arms crossed. "I have to say," he said, "I'm verrry, verrry disappointed."

"Saibal's just filling the role that is expected of him," I said.

"Whatever," said Pius. "Ten bucks and I'll keep my mouth shut."

Saibal pulled a leather wallet out of his back pocket and gave Pius a ten-dollar bill.

At the supper table, Saibal asked if someone could pass the ketchup for his fried bologna.

"Your English is so good," yelled Dad.

"Bah-gah!" yelled Gord.

Nan put another slice of bologna on Saibal's plate. "Look at him. He's skin and bones."

He was anything but. Saibal had broad shoulders, a full, round face—he was the picture of health.

Pius passed Saibal the ketchup. "You know, Saibal," he said, "what you're eating there is pretty rare. It's not very often a hunter comes across the wild bologna. Fierce creatures, they are. They'd bite the hand right off ya."

Saibal laughed. "Go on wit' ya, b'y. We all knows this bologna was sliced off the Maple Leaf Big Stick."

There was a collective gasp.

"He's a bloody Newfoundlander!" said Shelagh.

"He took advantage of my good nature!" said Nan.

"He ate all the tea buns!" said Dad.

"Bah-gah!" yelled Gord.

Saibal just kept eating. That's how good fried bologna is.

"He was just filling the role that was expected of him," I said.

Mom walked in in her dressing gown. "Who's this?"

"Barry's new friend," said Dad. "He's a real little scoundrel."

Mom sat down. "So they're two peas in a pod, then."

Nan jabbed a bony finger in Saibal's direction. "I made trifle for dessert. And you, young man, are getting one scoop. Just like everyone else."

"Just like everyone else, eh?" said Saibal. "Sounds good to me."

★

I walked Saibal to the bus stop.

"Sorry about that. It's like they've never seen a brown person before."

"Well, there aren't a lot of visible minorities in this city."

I wrapped my arm around his shoulder. "I bet by the time we're twenty, St. John's will look like a rainbow."

"In case you haven't noticed," said Saibal, "brown isn't a color of the rainbow."

"Neither is white."

"I bet you turn red in the summer, though," he said.

"Fair point," I said

Saibal looked at his watch. "We have ten minutes before the bus comes. Want to go get up to no good?"

"Sure," I said. "Let's go throw rocks at my school's windows."

We threw assorted stones and pebbles, but nothing broke the glass.

"This is ridiculous," said Saibal. "What if there was a fire inside? You'd never break out."

"They don't care," I said. "This place is like a prison. I'm surprised there are no iron bars."

We stood back and took in the red brick building.

"I suppose if there was a fire, we would just *open* the window," I said.

"Yeah," said Saibal. "They're still a bunch of bastards, though."

We walked back to the bus stop.

"What's *your* school like, Saibal?"

He kicked a pebble with his shoe. "White."

I laughed. "Who paints a school white?"

"The school isn't white," said Saibal. "The people are."

I picked up the pebble and dropped it in a random mailbox. "All of them?"

He nodded. "Yup."

He started hopping over the cracks in the sidewalk. "Step on a crack, break your mother's back."

I joined in. "It's always the mothers," I said. "I feel bad for them."

"Good point," he said. "Let's change it to father."

"How about brothers?" I said. "*Older* brothers."

We stomped on every crack.

Saibal laughed. "Poor Pius."

We slowed down and caught our breath.

"Sometimes I make brown jokes," said Saibal.

I looked over at him. "You do?"

He nodded. "It's better if I make them first. Doesn't hurt as much."

It was an interesting strategy. *Maybe*, I thought, *I should try it with my face.*

"The kids think I'm cool and funny when I make fun

of myself. But there's this one kid, Freddie Fudge. I'll never win him over. He's been to the office six times for calling me a Paki. He doesn't say it out loud anymore. But I hear it, you know?"

"It's called telepathy," I said.

Damian Clarke was a master.

"Do you have a bully?" asked Saibal.

I pointed to my face. "Duh."

We kept walking.

"Maybe we could put an ad in the paper," I said. "Like they did in that movie *Desperately Seeking Susan*. You know, the one with Madonna? We could say, 'Desperately Seeking Brown Kids,' and maybe you'd find a friend."

Saibal smiled. "That's okay, Finbar. I already have a friend."

I hoped he meant me.

We sat on the curb under the Route 12 sign. Saibal flicked an ant off my jeans.

"My mom has the baby blues," I said. "That's why she was in her dressing gown."

"That's too bad," said Saibal.

"Yeah," I said.

The Metrobus rounded the corner.

"See ya tomorrow, buddy," I said.

"See ya, Finbar."

★

I popped into Gord's room before going to my own. He was asleep but I whispered to him anyway. "I won't see you after school tomorrow. I have a performance at the nursing home. It's important. This could be my big break. You understand, right?"

He let one rip. It was long and wet and bubbly. I took it as a yes.

★

Saibal and I walked against the wind to the One Step Closer to God Nursing Home. Our hoods were up and our hands were stuffed in our pockets.

"I'm froze to death," said Saibal.

"Me too," I said.

As we moved out of the downtown area, row houses became detached homes and the steepness of the roads leveled out. We made our way up Portugal Cove Road and when we reached Elizabeth Avenue, we stopped at Regatta Ford to warm up. In the corner of the showroom, there was a candy machine. Saibal put in a quarter and twisted the knob. I put my hand at the bottom of the chute and collected the colored sour candy. We ate them in a Ford Crown Victoria. Red food dye came off on my fingers, so I wiped them on the leather interior.

Saibal was in the driver's seat playing with the steering wheel.

"Oh, shit," I said, looking out the back window. "It's the cops!"

Saibal grabbed the wheel and put his foot on the gas. He made car noises while I held the Jesus bar and said, "Burn rubber! The pigs are gaining on us."

Saibal bounced around on his seat, his eyes straight ahead. "Why did you have to kill him, Finbar? He was your big brother."

"That blackmailer was no brother of mine," I said. "I promised I'd get that ten bucks back and I did."

"But did you have to rip out his insides and step dance on them?" Saibal said. "It was a bit cruel, even for you."

"He got what he deserved," I said.

"Oh no," said Saibal. "Up ahead! It's Deadman's Pond."

"Step on the brakes!" I yelled.

"They're not working," he cried.

We tumbled about in our seats as the car went over the cliff. Saibal died with his head on the horn. I died laughing.

"Ahem."

A car salesman was standing by Saibal's open window.

"His parents are doctors," I said. "They asked us to pick out a luxury sedan on their behalf."

The man opened the door. "Out."

We put up our hoods and went back out in the cold.

"Too bad Gord missed that," I said.

"Yeah," said Saibal. "He'd have pooped his pants."

"Literally," I said.

We continued up Portugal Cove past the Holiday Inn. The nursing home was in the distance.

"I hope O'Flaherty shows up," I said.

"I'm sure he will," said Saibal.

"I'm nervous," I said.

"You could always wait for the September auditions," said Saibal.

"I can't disappoint God," I said. "He gave me a sign, you know."

"I'm sure he'd understand," said Saibal.

"What about you, Saibal?" I said. "Do you believe in God?"

"I believe in a few," said Saibal. "My favorite is Shiva. He's the god of destruction."

"Maybe you can pray to him the next time we're throwing rocks at the school window," I said. "It'd be nice for the glass to break for once."

"He only destroys evil," said Saibal.

"School's evil," I said.

"True," said Saibal. "I'll see what I can do."

Patsy greeted us at the nursing home. "They're waiting for you."

I took Billy Walsh's tap shoes out of my backpack. They were two sizes too big.

"Here," said Patsy, crumpling up the *Evening Telegram*. Saibal shoved the balled-up newspaper into the toes.

"Perfect," I said, rocking back and forth.

The Last Chance Saloon was packed with old people sitting on plastic garden chairs. Uneven Steven waved from the front row. I clicked toward him, waving and winking to the oldies as I passed them by. Saibal followed behind.

"Hi, Steven," I said.

Steven looked beyond me.

"'Allo, Saibal."

"You two know each other?" I said.

"Saibal organized a sock drive for the Harbour Light Centre last year," said Steven. "I had warm plates of meat all winter."

"He means feet," said Saibal.

"I know what he means," I said. "I'm not a garden tool."

"Fool?" said Saibal.

"Bingo!" said Steven.

"Bingo?" said Edie from the second row. "I thought we were here for a show."

"And that you are, Eeds," I said.

I stretched my arms over my head and bent from left to right.

"Nice to see you warming up," said Uneven Steven. "I'd have never kept up with Jagger without a few pre-show stretches."

"You played with the Stones?" said Saibal.

"Keith Richards had the sniffles," said Steven. "I was his fill-in."

"Unbelievable," said Saibal, sneaking me a wink.

I smiled. It was nice of him to play along.

I was swinging my leg over the back of a garden chair when the elusive Father O'Flaherty walked in. I say *elusive* because Father O'Flaherty was a man who kept a low profile, and elusive means hard to find. It's what Mr. McGraw called me whenever my homework was due. Father O'Flaherty had been in town for almost six months now but none of the parishioners really knew him. Our old parish priest, Father Molloy, was out and about all the time—at Tim Hortons having a chat and a double-double, down on George Street having a pint of "medicinal" Guinness, in Bannerman Park sunbathing in his Speedo. Father O'Flaherty, on the other hand, only made himself available during official religious duties. He did spend a lot of time with the Full Tilt Dancers, though. Apparently, like me, he was quite taken with *Riverdance*. He even flew to Dublin to see one of their shows. According to Billy Walsh, it was O'Flaherty's goal to make the Full Tilt Dancers the best Irish step dance troupe in Canada. *If that's the case,* I thought, *he'll definitely need the likes of me.* I clicked over to him.

"Fancy meeting you here."

He looked me up and down. "Do I know you?"

"You will soon," I said.

"Who knit ya?" he asked.

"My conception had nothing to do with needles and wool," I said. "The tools of the trade were more, how shall I put it, biological. But to answer your question, my parents are Brendan and Margaret Squires. From York Street."

He scowled. "So you're the infamous Finbar Squires."

I put out my hand. "The one and only."

He didn't shake it.

"Father Molloy told me about you. You're the youngster who punched a hole though the confessional screen."

"In one blow," I said. "But my talents don't stop there."

I nodded toward my tap shoes, then raised my eyebrows.

"You're a dancer?"

I smiled. "Some might call me the best-kept secret in the dance world."

He looked intrigued. "Really?"

I put a finger to the side of my nose and walked away.

Uneven Steven gave me a thumbs-up. "Good luck with the ol' Jack Palance."

"That means dance," said Saibal.

"Just so you know," I said, "Cockney is my second language. So I don't need *you* acting like you're some kind of goddamn translator."

Saibal elbowed Steven in the arm. "Someone's getting themselves into a real cream puff."

"That means huff," said Steven.

"I knew what he meant," I said, even though I hadn't.

I stood on the X and looked around. "Music, please."

"Performers usually bring their own equipment," called Patsy.

"But this is the Last Chance—I mean, the special events room," I said. "How in God's name does it not have a sound system?"

"You think this place has money for a sound system?" she said.

I closed my eyes. *Focus, Squires, focus. What would Flatley do?*

A raspy and somewhat muffled voice rose from the crowd.

"Are you just going to stand there or what?"

I opened my eyes to see an old woman sneering at me through her oxygen mask.

"Take a chill pill, Darth."

Patsy wagged her finger at me. "You, young fella, are a disgrace."

So much for "We're not fussy, my duck. I'm sure you'll be delightful."

"I'm going back to my room," said a man in the front row. "*Land and Sea* is on."

"Me too," said another. "Tonight's episode is 'The Trouble with Beavers.'"

"Oooooh, beavers," everyone murmured.

"Wait," I said. "Don't go."

I looked to Buster and Edie for help. Buster gave me a wink and started *da-da-da*-ing the *Land and Sea* theme tune. Edie joined in. Soon the whole room was filled with song.

Uneven Steven caught my eye. "What are ya waiting for?" he growled. "Dance."

I pinned my arms to my sides and danced to the delightful ditty that filled Newfoundland homes on a weekly basis. It was a bit slow, but beggars can't be choosers. When they were done, I said, "Thanks, b'ys. I really appreciate it. How's about we do something faster this time?"

Edie started them off.

Beer, beer, beer, tiddly beer, beer, beer!

An Irish drinking song. Perfect.

A long time ago, way back in history,
When all there was to drink was nothin' but cups of tea,
Along came a man by the name of Charlie Mopps,
And he invented a wonderful drink and he made it out
of hops.

Everyone joined in. They swung their arms in unison.
I channeled my inner Flatley and kicked my legs high
in the air. The singing was so loud you couldn't even hear
the thuds as I landed. It was brilliant.

He must have been an admiral, a sultan, or a king,
And to his praises we shall always sing.
Look what he has done for us, he's filled us up with cheer!
Lord bless Charlie Mopps, the man who invented beer,
beer, beer,
Tiddly beer, beer, beer . . .

Buster caught my eye and threw me his cane. I caught
it with one hand and broke into the Charleston. Then I
twirled it like a baton and did my signature moonwalk.

It was time for my big finish. I landed the splits without the pain showing on my face. The room erupted in
cheers.

Uneven Steven wiped a tear from his eye.

Saibal started a standing ovation. It took a full six
minutes for everyone to get to their feet, but still.

I clicked my way over to Father O'Flaherty. "Well?"

"Well what?"

"How's about you invite me to join that troupe of yours?"

He laughed. "I don't think so. There's no room for temperamental divas in the Full Tilt Dancers."

My grip tightened around Buster's cane. "I'm going to tell my nan."

Father O'Flaherty looked amused. "And what's *she* going to do?"

I snorted. "What's she *not* going to do, more like."

"What's that supposed to mean?"

"My nan's almost a hundred," I said. "She'll be dead soon. Apparently she's willed it all to the church, but one word from me . . ."

O'Flaherty's brow furrowed. I moved my mouth toward his ear. "Mark my words. I *will* be in your dance troupe."

I turned on my heel and stormed out of the room. Out in the lobby, I swung Buster's cane like a baseball bat, knocking three table lamps to the floor. They smashed into a billion pieces.

Uneven Steven came barreling behind me.

"Bloomin' heck, Squire! Have you gone Patrick Swayze?"

In the distance, we heard a mass shuffling.

Steven grabbed the cane. "Make yourself scarce, Squire."

I ran like the wind to York Street.
Every click was a stab to the heart.

★

I sat on the floor and put my hand through the slats. I put my hand on Gord's arm and matched my breathing to his. I'd missed our bedtime song, so I wiped my eyes and sang:

Beer, beer, beer, tiddly beer, beer, beer . . .

CHAPTER SIX

I thrust the tap shoes into Billy Walsh's chest. "Here."

"How did it go?" he said.

"Swell."

He looked at his crotch. "Wish I could say the same."

"Were you thinking about God?" I said. "He likes to invade impure thoughts."

"It wasn't God," he said. "It was me mudder invading my underwear drawer. She found the *Playboy* and dragged me to confession."

"Jesus Murphy," I said. "What did Father O'Flaherty say?"

"He said he'd have to confiscate it but Mom had already burned it. He seemed disappointed."

"Better luck next time," I said.

When I walked into Mr. McGraw's class, he told me Mrs. Muckle wanted to see me. I walked into her office like I owned the place.

"Can't get enough of me, can you, Judes?"

She pointed at the chair across from her. "Sit."

She said she'd heard about the incident at the nursing home.

"I'm sorry it didn't go as planned, Barry, but you must control that temper of yours. Apparently you were so upset, you ran out of the home and accidentally knocked over three lamps."

"Who told you that?" I asked.

"Steven Morris."

"Steven who?"

"Steven Morris. You know, the homeless man?"

"Oh. Uneven Steven."

"Don't call him that," she said. "It's cruel."

"Cruel is having one leg longer than the other," I said. "Or a port-wine stain across your face."

"Oh, Barry," she said.

Her voice had gone soft and I wanted it hard again.

"It wasn't an accident," I said. "I whacked the lamps with a cane."

She sighed. "In any case, Steven has offered to replace them."

I clasped my hands behind my head and relaxed back. "Well, there you go," I said. "Problem solved."

"No," she said. "Problem *not* solved. That man doesn't have two pennies to rub together. You should be the one taking consequences for your actions. Not him."

"You know," I said, putting my feet up on her desk, "this incident is not a school issue, and quite frankly this conversation is starting to feel a little bit inappropriate."

She pushed my feet to the floor. "Father O'Flaherty felt it was his duty to inform me of your behavior. It takes a village, you know, Finbar."

"Oh, please. What does Father O'Flaherty know? He certainly doesn't know a good dancer when he sees one."

"Actually," she said, "it was your attitude that bothered him. He said your dancing has potential."

I sat up. "He did?"

She studied my face. "Why do you want this so bad, Barry?"

"Everyone wants to be known for something," I said.

She opened her mouth and closed it again.

"Go on," I said. "Tell me. What am I known for?"

The answer was written all over my face.

"Your humor. Your smarts. Your way with words."

I sighed. "In adult circles, perhaps. But with the other students?"

Again, she had no answer.

I stood up and leaned forward.

"You know exactly what I'm known for, Judes." I pointed to my cheek. "You're looking at it."

"Barry," she said. "Sit."

I sat back in my seat.

"Not there," she said. "At your desk."

I smiled. "*My* desk?"

"Your name's on it, isn't it?"

I sat down at the desk in the corner and ran my fingers along the *FTS* I'd scraped into the wood. Mrs. Muckle passed me a piece of paper.

"Father O'Flaherty's a reasonable man. Write him a letter. Plead your case."

I nodded. "Thank you, Judes."

I began.

My dearest Father O'Flaherty,

Some of the greatest artists in the world are the temper and mental type. Ozzy Osbourne bit the head off a bat live onstage. Van Gogh cut his own ear off. It kind of puts things in perspective, doesn't it? When you think about it, my behavior was nothing more than a little tantrum, and let's face it, it was kind of justified. I mean, how can you have a musical performance without music? But I—

"Judes? What's the word you use when you want to change the subject? Begins with *d*? Sounds like *digest*?"

"Digress," she said.

But I digress. This dancing malarkey is about more than being temper and mental. It's about being chosen. You see, Father O, I received a message from God himself. He told me to dance. There was an almighty glow and everything. So you see, you don't really have a choice in all of this. I was meant to be a Full Tilt Dancer. God said so.

Sincerely and with the utmost of respect and gratitude,

Finbar T. Squires

Mrs. Muckle read it over.

"It's *temperamental*, not temper and mental," she said. "And don't call him Father O. It's the height of rudeness."

"Other than that," I said, "is it good?"

She sighed. "Well. It's passionate."

"It's like they say," I said. "Go big or go home. And speaking of going home—I'm feeling a bit emotionally drained. I think I might call it a day."

She passed me my schoolbag. "Go to class, Barry."

★

Mr. McGraw kicked me out of class. It wasn't my fault everyone jumped on their chairs. I was sure I saw two rats scurrying across the floor with foam around their mouths. Turns out I'd just imagined them. I blamed McGraw. His talk about compound adjectives was mind-numbing. As for my peers, why should I be blamed for their over-reaction? They could have just stayed seated with their legs up, like me. I left on a high note, though, passing in a copy of my letter to Father O'Flaherty as my persuasive essay. I said I'd be happy with a B-plus if he couldn't find it within his cold, dead heart to give me an A. It's amazing how many shades of purple and red the human face can turn. It's really quite mind-blowing.

I managed to sit through my other classes without causing a disruption. Mostly because I'd mastered the art of dreaming with my eyes open. In science, I was Father O'Flaherty's lead dancer and by the end of last period, I was on stage with Michael Flatley. All in all it was a successful day, even without a saltwater taffy reward.

On my way home, I went to the corner of Cochrane and Duckworth because Uneven Steven hadn't been there before school.

"Did you sleep in this morning?" I asked.

He nodded. "I was up late last night replacing the broken lamps."

"Where did you buy them?" I asked.

"I said replacing, not buying."

"So you robbed them?"

"I may be a lot of things," said Steven, "but I'm no tea leaf."

"So you borrowed them?"

"I went to the dump," he said. "They're ugly and cracked but they work."

"Thanks, Steven. You're a pal."

I went home and got Gord. Saibal was at the war memorial with two birch beers and a Pixy Stix for Gord.

"He can't have that," I said.

"It's just a bit of sugar," said Saibal.

He ripped the paper straw with his teeth. "Open up, Gord."

Gord tipped his head back and opened wide.

"Oh my God!" I said. "A tooth!"

"It looks like a Chiclet," said Saibal.

I ran my finger along the pearly-white eruption.

"He's growing up," I said.

"His first tooth," said Saibal. "Let's take him to Bannerman Park to celebrate."

We arrived at the park to find the swings wound over the top bar.

"Some people have too much time on their hands," I said.

"Now what are we going to do?" said Saibal.

"We could go throw rocks at my school again," I said.

"Why don't we complain to the city," said Saibal. "These swings are their responsibility."

"Better yet," I said, "let's take it up with the lieutenant governor."

"Good idea," said Saibal.

Government House was just across the street. We crossed Bannerman Road and headed toward the grand brick building.

"My parents got invited to the garden party last year," said Saibal. "Someone thought my dad was a server and handed him an empty glass."

"That's the height of rudeness," I said.

"It was a good party, though," said Saibal. "There was a band and everything."

"My nan has always wanted to go," I said, "but I think you gotta be someone to get an invite."

"Your nan's someone," said Saibal.

"It's okay," I said. "She doesn't have a big hat anyway."

Saibal stayed with Gord while I climbed the stairs and rapped on the door. A maid in black-and-white uniform answered.

"I'd like to speak to the lieutenant governor," I said.

"Do you have an appointment?" she asked.

"I most certainly do."

"Your name?"

"Finbar T. Squires. The *T* is for Turlough. I'm telling you this because a highfalutin middle name such as mine is an indication of the grand family from which I was born into. We really are quite the bunch of someones."

She stared at me blankly.

Gord rat-tat-tat-tatted like a machine gun.

"Babies are so uncouth," I said.

She turned back into the building.

"Don't forget," I said. "Turlough. Spelled with an *o-u-g-h* but pronounced like 'lock.' It means 'dry lake,' which is an oxymoron."

The door slammed in my face.

"That went well," said Saibal.

A few moments later, the door opened again. A man in a gray suit stood in the doorway.

"Finbar Turlough Squires?"

I was amazed. Namedropping really worked. Even if it was your own.

I put out my hand. "The one and only. And you, sir, must be the lieutenant governor of this very fine province I'm proud to call home."

The man took my hand. "I'm his private secretary. You can call me Gord."

My eyes lit up. "He's Gord too," I said, pointing at the stroller.

"A fine Scottish name," said the man.

"My mother felt it was important to acknowledge the long line of Scottish royalty on her father's side," I said.

In reality, Gord was named after Gordon Lightfoot. Apparently Dad agreed because her second favorite singer was Elvis.

Big Gord looked at Saibal. "And what's your name?"

"Saibal," said Saibal. "It's Indian."

"An Irishman, a Scotsman, and an Indian," said Big Gord. "You three should walk into a bar."

"The past, present, and the future walked into a bar," I said.

"Let me guess," said Big Gord. "It was tense."

We all laughed. Except Gord. He knew nothing about grammar.

"So," I said. "Where's the big man himself? We kind of have a bone to pick with him."

"He's in a meeting," said Big Gord. "Is there anything I can help you with?"

I pointed across to Bannerman Park. "Some yahoo has swung the swings around the top pole and we can't reach them."

He went inside and grabbed a cap. It was navy with a braid above the peak.

"You're going to help us?" I said.

"Why wouldn't I?" asked Big Gord.

"Because you're an important someone," I said.

He smiled. "I hear you're quite the someone too."

Big Gord stretched his arms in front of us as cars whizzed by.

"Okay," he said. "It's safe to go."

We parked Gord near the swings. A seagull landed on the canopy of the stroller.

"Yah!" yelled Big Gord.

"Bah!" yelled Little Gord.

The seagull flew away.

Big Gord stood in his suit whacking the swings with a stick. I told him how my nan had always wanted to go to the garden party and about Saibal's dad being mistaken for a server.

"Not that there's anything wrong with being a server," said Saibal. "It's just that people make assumptions."

"Do you think if the whole world was blind, there'd be no prejudice?" I asked.

Big Gord unraveled one swing and moved to the next.

"To quote Thomas Hardy," he said, "'There is a condition worse than blindness, and that is, seeing something that isn't there.'"

"What does that mean?" asked Saibal.

"It means that sometimes people see what they want to see," said Big Gord. "Like differences."

"Why would people want to see differences?" I said.

Big Gord unraveled the last swing. "Maybe it helps them feel superior."

He put down the stick and put a hand on Saibal's shoulder. "What they don't realize," he said, "is that they may *feel* superior but they *look* like pompous twits."

He gave a little bow. "Good day, boys."

We watched him walk away.

"He's a nice man," said Saibal.

"Bah-gah!" yelled Gord.

★

At suppertime, Mom came to the table fully dressed and ready to eat. She doled fish and brewis onto everyone's plate.

"I have some news," she said.

"Good God," said Pius. "You're not pregnant, are ya?"

Mom gave a little laugh. "No."

Dad put his arm around her.

She cleared her throat. "A few weeks back I went to the doctor. He gave me some antidepressants. I'm starting to feel better. I'm sorry for being so absent."

It sounded rehearsed. I wondered if she'd been practicing all morning.

"I have some news too," said Nan.

"Good God," said Pius. "You're not pregnant, are ya?"

Nan laughed. "Go 'way with ya, Pius. You're as foolish as an odd sock."

She looked at me and smiled. "Father O'Flaherty called. He said you can join the troupe on a trial basis."

I grinned. "I knew he'd see things my way."

"I have news too," said Shelagh.

"What is it?" asked Mom.

Shelagh looked to the table. "I want Pius to ask."

Pius looked up from his fish and brewis. "What?"

"I want you to ask about my news. The same way you asked everyone else."

As soon as he asked it, we understood.

Mom's voice was a growl. "You silly girl."

"What about Bob?" said Shelagh. "Is he silly too?"

Dad put his head in his hands. "Just what we need. Another mouth to feed."

The concern about money surprised me. The last time I checked, sex before marriage was against our religion. Then again, so was taking the Lord's name in vain and Lord Jumpin' Jesus, we did enough of that.

When Shelagh started crying, I took Gord upstairs. "Well, one good thing's come out of it," I whispered. "Mom can't call you her little blunder anymore."

★

Shelagh cried for three days. "There goes my studies at Memorial."

"And whose fault is that?" said Mom.

Dad, who was still in shock, could only nod in agreement.

Nan, on the other hand, moved on. "Shelagh's not the first pregnant teen," she said, "and she won't be the last."

I overheard Pius ask Shelagh if Bob was a good guy and when she said yes, he said, "Good."

I didn't care either way. I just hoped Mom's happy pills were extra strength.

★

A few nights later, just as things were settling down, all hell broke loose. Pius and his hockey friends were in the basement kicking the crap out of each other in a makeshift boxing ring while the rest of us were upstairs watching *The Price Is Right*. An overexcited contestant in a Hawaiian shirt was losing his shit over a game of Plinko when there was a knock on the door. I peeked out the window. "It's a guy with a big schnoz." Shelagh's face turned red, then white, then green.

"It's okay, love," said Mom. "Invite him in. We'll have to meet him sometime." My poor mother. If she had a white flag, she'd have probably waved it.

Shelagh went to the door but never came back.

"Don't worry," I said. "I got this."

Just as I was positioning myself behind the slightly open front door, Pius and his friends came upstairs. Pius said, "When is a door not a door?"

The answer was "when it's ajar," but I didn't respond. I had work to do. "Shush," I said. "I'm eavesdropping."

I reported back to the living room in a loud whisper.

"He says he hasn't told his parents yet."

"She told him he has to."

"He says he's scared."

"She said tough shit."

"He said maybe she should make this go away."

"She said it's her body and she'll damn well decide what to do with it."

"He says of course it's her decision. He's sorry."

"She says she doesn't want to fight."

"He says he doesn't either but he can't tell his parents."

"She says he has to."

"He says he's sorry but he can't do it. His parents will kill him."

Pius pushed me out of the way. "Not if I kill him first."

With the door now wide open, I was able to give a full play-by-play.

"Pius just punched Bob in the face. I think Bob just called Pius a rubberducker. Shelagh's saying the Hail Mary."

Dad, Mom, and Nan ran to the door. I grabbed Gord from Nan's arms. "This is gonna be good, Gord," I said. "Real good."

I gave the gathering neighbors a little wave as I settled onto the front steps with Gord. Pius and Bob were squaring off again. The adults were saying, "Stop this right now!" At least I think they were—it was hard to hear them over the chants of "Kill him!" coming from Pius's friends. Pius was scuffing his foot like a bull about to charge when Shelagh blocked him from Bob, saying, "Please don't kill the father of my child." The neighbors gasped. Mom, suddenly aware that the neighbors were watching, started applauding. "Aren't they marvelous?" she said. "The best youth acting troupe in town."

Nan herded everyone back into the house, where Shelagh wiped the blood off Bob's face with his own shirt—I don't think she loved him enough to use her own. Nan put the kettle on and sliced up one of her boiled raisin cakes. Dad snorted. "The best youth acting troupe in town." We all laughed. Even Mom. The hockey boys said Nan's cake was the best they'd had. Nan beamed. When the teapot was drained, Pius invited Bob downstairs to check out the makeshift boxing ring. He said he figured Bob could use some pointers. Bob said he'd like that. He also said he'd tell his parents that night. It's amazing what a punch in the face, a cup of tea, and a slice of boiled raisin cake can do.

★

I probably shouldn't have broadcast it, but when I saw the petition, I had no choice. It was posted on the lunchroom wall and as I approached it, a kid in fifth grade said, "Sorry, but I had to sign it. Herpes is very contagious. Especially when it's on your face."

I looked around. Damian Clarke and Thomas Budgell were doubled over. With all eyes on me, I said, "This practical joke has come at a very difficult time. My teenaged sister is pregnant. My family is in crisis. I'd appreciate prayers, not stares."

A hush fell over the room. After all, premarital sex was against our religion. For the rest of the day, I was left alone. I had successfully managed to get the focus off my face and onto the shame of my family. All in all, it was a good day.

★

After school Saibal and I pushed Gord up Signal Hill.

"When's the baby coming?" he asked.

"September. Shelagh's three months already."

Saibal pinched Gord's cheeks. "You're gonna be second fiddle soon, buddy boy."

"No one will ever replace Gord," I said.

At the top of the hill, we sat on a wall overlooking the harbor. Saibal held Gord tightly in his lap and the wind whipped at our faces. The basilica stood out in the distance, surrounded by the old buildings and colorful houses of downtown. A coast guard boat made its way out through the Narrows.

"We're lucky to live here, aren't we, Saibal?"

"We sure are," he said.

I wondered what time it was.

"My first dance lesson is soon," I said.

"But you don't have a uniform," said Saibal.

"Whenever I bring it up, Dad tells me to hold my tongue," I said. "I brought pennies to tape to my shoes, though."

"You can't do that," said Saibal. "It's very unprofessional."

"What else am I supposed to do?" I asked.

"How 'bout this," he said. "You go to practice and promise O'Flaherty the money will be there by the end of class. In the meantime, I'll drop Gord off, get the bus home, grab my bank card, get the bus back, go to the Royal Bank, get you some money, and meet you at the BIS for the end of class."

"Really?" I said.

I was stunned. A bank card at age twelve?

He put an arm around my shoulder. "What are friends for?"

We headed back down the winding, steep Signal Hill Road.

Gord, who rarely got fussy, got fussy.

When we got to a relatively straight bit of sidewalk, I said, "I have an idea."

I gave Saibal the stroller and ran ahead.

"Okay," I said, turning around and bracing myself. "Let him go."

Saibal laughed. "What? I can't do that."

"Yes, you can," I said. "I'll catch him. Don't worry."

Saibal shrugged and let go. Gord shrieked as the stroller sped down the incline.

"I gotcha, Gord!" I said. "I gotcha!"

The stroller raced toward me. When it got close, I reached out and grabbed Gord by the waist.

"Bah!" he yelled.

Saibal caught up to us.

"He wants to go again," I said.

At the next straight stretch of sidewalk, we switched. I trusted Saibal to catch him and he did.

At the bottom of the hill, I said, "Nan made raisin squares this morning. She'll probably only give you one, seeing as you're not a refugee anymore."

Saibal tightened Gord's seatbelt. "Oh, don't you worry," he said. "I'll get at least three squares off your nan."

"How do you plan on doing that?" I asked.

"I'm gonna charm the pants right off her."

"Please don't," I said. "She'll catch her death."

Saibal took Gord home and I went to the BIS. Father O'Flaherty said that as a man of the cloth, he had no choice but to have faith in my promise of money, so he gave me the uniform. I put on the Newfoundland tartan pants, a crisp white shirt, and the tartan vest. I thought I'd feel like a dancer, but the only thing I felt like was a leprechaun, not that's there's anything wrong with that.

Then I put on the shoes.

They were brand-new, not like Billy's, which were faded and worn. These were shiny and black and the silver taps clicked like no penny could.

I strutted out of the bathroom and down the hall.

Click.

Click.

Clickity-click.

I entered the practice room with my chest puffed out and took my place amongst the evenly spaced rows of dancers. Father O'Flaherty cleared his throat. When I looked up, he pointed to the door. "The beginners are down the hall, second door on the right."

I smiled. "Give me a couple of weeks. I'll be back."

As I walked down the hall, I chuckled at the thought of me being a beginner. Ha! A beginner doesn't watch *Riverdance* two times in a row. Especially when the running time is seventy-one minutes. I mean, that's dedication.

I walked into the second door on the right. Some of the dancers were barely up to my knees. The tallest barely reached my shoulders.

The teacher introduced himself. "I'm Brian."

"I know who you are," I said. He was in the grade below me at school.

We practiced pointing our toes by dipping them in the Atlantic Ocean.

"Brrrr," said Brian.

The little fellas were having a grand time.

But I wasn't *brrrr*-ing. I was *grrrr*-ing.

We skipped across the room to the Pacific.

"Ahhhh, much warmer," said Brian.

"No offense, Brian," I said. "But these infantile shenanigans are beneath me."

A moment later I was peering through the window on O'Flaherty's door. They were dancing to "Mari-Mac." With my hands on my hips, I leapt into the room. I spread my legs as wide as I could and thrust my chin in the air. *This'll show 'em. The bastards.* I landed with a thud and continued dancing, tapping in and out through the rows of stunned-yet-amazed boys. Always considerate and thinking of others, I timed my kicks so as not to cause testicular injury. At the end of the third row, Father O'Flaherty blocked my way, but not even his physical presence could stop me. With my arms pinned tight to my sides, I step danced in place.

"Are you done?" he said.

My voice was breathless. "Does it look like it?"

His jaw hardened. "You have two choices," he said. "Go back to the beginners' room or go home."

"You've put me in a difficult position," I panted.

"I'll make it easy for you," he said. "Go home."

I was kind of relieved. My plates of meat were killing me. Things would be better next week when I'd be feeling more refreshed.

I clicked my way to the door.

"Finbar?" he said.

I paused. Maybe this was where he'd tell me I showed potential, where my hard work would pay off.

"Don't come back," he said.

My face fell. "What?"

"You can leave the uniform in the cloakroom."

My jaw hardened. "You, sir, are a dream killer. A hope dasher. A spirit squasher."

"Perhaps, Squires," he said, "you'd be better suited to

the local acting troupe. You seem to have a flair for the dramatic."

I didn't disagree. I probably *would* excel in theater. But that was beside the point. I refused to be fooled by his flattery.

"Yes, Father," I said. "I do have a flair for the dramatic. So allow me to leave you with some parting words."

I cleared my throat.

"Dimes are silver, pennies are brass, why does your face look like your ass?"

The boys roared with laughter. O'Flaherty sputtered. Fearing that he might need CPR, I left. It wasn't very Christian, refusing to give the kiss of life to a man of God, but neither was crushing the hopes and dreams of a twelve-year-old boy.

I left the uniform in a pile on the cloakroom floor and went outside to wait for Saibal. He'd probably be on his way back by now. I felt bad about the wasted journey. I'd suggest blowing the money at Caines to make up for it.

★

"Don't listen to the likes of Father O'Fart-ity," said Saibal. "He wouldn't know talent if it hit him in the face."

"I know," I said. "It still hurts, though."

"Let's drown our sorrows with a couple of birch beers."

"And some chips and a Caramel Log?"

"Why not?" said Saibal.

We took our stash to the bandstand in Bannerman Park to shelter from the rain, drizzle, and fog. We sat on our knees to keep from freezing our arses off and pulled our hoods up over our heads.

"I like this weather," said Saibal.

"Me too," I said. "It makes me feel alive."

"Warm days are boring," said Saibal. "It's the same outside as it is in. But on damp days, the cold on your cheeks lasts for ages and when your mudder touches them with the back of her hand, she makes you a cup of tea with bucketloads of sugar."

"Sometimes," I said, "when the fog is as thick as pea soup, I go downtown and walk in the alleys and imagine getting murdered by a serial killer with a machete. It's never happened, though."

"I'll come with you next time," he said. "We can get killed together."

"That'd be nice," I said.

A seagull landed on the bandstand steps. Saibal threw it a chip.

I closed one eye and stared into the opening of my birch beer. I had no reason to do this. I already knew it was pink.

"How about we go to the nursing home?" said Saibal.

It was the perfect suggestion. A dance with the oldies was just what I needed.

"You, sir," I said, "are like a blast of Newfoundland weather."

Saibal grinned. "I make you feel alive?"

"No," I said. "You're as thick as pea soup."

Saibal threw a chip at me. It bounced off my nose.

"Come on," I said. "Let's go have ourselves a good old knees-up."

★

We sat in the Last Chance Saloon with Buster, Edie, and a handful of others. They'd been in the lobby when I'd arrived but as soon as I said, "Let's dance," they got to their feet and followed me down the hall like I was the Pied Piper of Hamelin, except they weren't rats and I didn't have a flute.

Buster tapped his cane against the floor. "Are we going to have a song and dance or what?"

"Absolutely," I said. "But first—"

Saibal and I pooled our change together and set about taping coins to the soles of everyone's shoes, including our own. Once we got everyone to their feet, we moved to the middle of the room, where we had a good old-fashioned Newfoundland kitchen party. Our shoes sounded way better than the ones I'd been wearing earlier. It must have been the acoustics of the room.

We sang "Lukey's Boat" and "Rattlin' Bog." We tapped, shuffled, boogied, and waltzed. Edie's hands were like two chunks of ice, but I held them anyway as we stepped side to side, clicking in unison. More people came and joined in. Saibal was spinning someone around in a wheelchair and a little old lady in orthopedic shoes was doing a slow but impressive Charleston. They formed a circle around me, and Buster said, "Take it away, Barry!" I did the fastest step dance in the history of man and my face wore the world's smuggest look, and I thought, "If O'Flaherty could see me now."

CHAPTER SEVEN

There was a freak snowstorm in April that lasted three days. It came over Easter, and on Good Friday I suggested we bond as a family by painting eggs but everyone had an excuse. Shelagh said she couldn't even look at an egg without throwing up, Pius said decorating eggs was for morons, and the adults were watching *Jesus Christ Superstar*. The only person mildly interested in painting eggs was Gord, but he had no fine motor skills. I asked Mom if she'd managed to buy any Easter chocolate before the storm. She said no but all was not lost because at least she had a turkey.

"All is not lost?" I screamed. "If I don't get a Mr. Solid, there'll be hell to pay."

The Easter Bunny had been bringing me a Mr. Solid ever since I had teeth.

Mary Magdalene was on the TV singing "Everything's Alright" to Jesus. Mom joined in and sang it to me.

"Everything is *not* all right!" I screamed.

"Bah!" yelled Gord from Dad's lap.

I stormed into the kitchen and looked in the fridge. There were four eggs left. One for each kid. I found a magic marker and wrote our names on them: Pius, Preggo, Finbar, and Gord. I went outside and threw them at the window. That'll teach 'em.

The snow was deep but I had on my big snow boots, so I trudged all the way from York to Springdale. I threw snowballs at the Harbour Light Centre till somebody answered the door.

"Uneven Steven, please," I said.

"Whom shall I say is calling?" asked the man in the doorway.

"The one he calls Squire," I said, to add an air of mystery.

A moment later Steven appeared.

"Come in, Squire," he said. "We're about to have a cup of Rosy Lee."

I followed him to a big kitchen and joined a group of men at an oversized table. A man with a tattooed face put a Mr. Solid in front of me. "Here ya go, fella."

"You, sir," I said, "are a scholar and a gentleman."

I took off the wrapping and bit the ears off. Turns out, the center had received a box of donated Easter chocolate.

"Listen, fellas," I said. "The Easter Bunny's been a bit distracted this year 'cause her teenage daughter is preggers. How's about I shovel the driveway in exchange for seven Cadbury cream eggs?"

"Deal," said the man with the tattooed face. "But I'll help. It's a big job."

We went outside and as we shoveled side by side he told me he'd just been released from the pen.

"Six years for armed robbery," he said. "Whatever you do, kid, don't do drugs."

When we got inside, a man with a long, yellowed face filled a Sobeys bag with way more than seven cream eggs.

"Thanks, buddy," I said.

Uneven Steven made me hot chocolate to warm up and spoke to the group about the hardships of being a performer

"I hear ya," I said. "I think I've got a blister developing on my big toe."

Then he told us about the time a photo of him ended up in *Rolling Stone* magazine.

"It was '79," he said. "My buddy Joe Strummer pulled me up onstage during one of their gigs. Let's just say my dance moves stole the show."

He got up and limped to the kitchen sink. The tattooed man gave me a wink. I felt bad for Steven, with his made-up stories. I'm sure he did wonderful things in his life. Why didn't he share *them* instead?

I followed Steven to the sink and whispered, "Why would someone tattoo their face? I'd do anything to get rid of this mess on mine."

"Where would I be if I got my leg fixed?" he said. "It was what I was known for. Like Jagger's lips. In my opinion, you should stick with what you're born with. Imagine if Freddie Mercury got his teeth fixed. It could have changed the whole structure of his mouth and affected the way he sang."

I stuck out my front teeth and sang "Another One Bites the Dust." It sounded terrible.

"Give us a dance then, Barry," said one of the men.

The man with the tattooed face lifted me onto the table. Another played the fiddle. It felt good to entertain down-and-outs. I hoped I'd added a little something to their humdrum lives.

★

On the way home, I stopped at the Hanrahans. Mrs. Hanrahan's husband killed himself because he'd grown up in the Mount Cashel Orphanage. The news had come out years earlier that the Christian Brothers had been abusing the boys. It was enough to make Mom stop going to church. Dad still went, though. He took us with him while Mom stayed home and cooked the Sunday dinner. I felt bad for Mrs. Hanrahan. Her kids were the kind you'd see out in their pajamas at the crack of dawn, pulling up the neighbors' potted plants.

When she answered the door, I said, "You get out to the stores this week?" And when she said no, I gave her the contents of the Sobeys bag, minus the seven Cadbury eggs. "Happy Easter."

"Thank you, Finbar," she said. "Between you and Mrs. O'Brien, I'm all set. She brought a turkey over this morning."

I said, "This storm's screwing everybody over," but truth be told, she'd have struggled regardless.

When I got home, Dad was cleaning the window. I could barely see him through the snow, which had begun to fall quite heavily again.

"I don't need this, Barry," he said. "I've got enough problems."

"What do you mean, problems?" I said. "Mom's on happy pills and so what, Shelagh's pregnant. It's not like she's been diagnosed with cancer or anything."

I had hoped that would put things in perspective for him. Instead, his face turned purple.

"Barry. Do you ever think about things before you say them?"

"Well, duh. You have to think in order to form words, otherwise you'd say nothing at all."

I continued toward the house.

"By the way," I said, holding up the Sobeys bag, "I saved Easter."

★

The power went out on Saturday, but it turned out to be the best day ever. We sat around the fire and when we got hungry, we put a skillet in the flames and fried bologna, and when we played Scrabble, they even scored my made-up words, and during Trivial Pursuit, when Dad asked the Arts and Literature question "Who painted *The Birth of Venus*?", Shelagh placed a hand on her tummy and Mom reached over and said, "Any kicks yet?" and Shelagh smiled and her eyes went teary.

When the power came back on, my eyes went teary too.

★

The adults slept in on Easter morning because it was too snowy for church. Not that Mom would have gone, but

Dad and Nan would have dragged us there. I took Gord downstairs and placed a cream egg in each of our spots on the table. I put one on the tray of Gord's high chair. "This is symbolic because you've only got one tooth," I said. "But don't worry, I'll give you a lick of the center."

At ten o'clock they were still asleep, so I shouted, "Jesus rose from the dead today. The least you bastards can do is get out of bed!"

A few moments later, they appeared.

"Look," I said. "The Easter Bunny came."

Nan tightened the belt on her dressing gown. "Oh, Barry. How lovely."

"A single egg," said Pius, biting his in half. "How delightful."

A splodge of yolk dropped onto his chest.

Shelagh held her stomach. "I think I'm going to be sick."

Mom nodded at Dad. "Go get the Zellers bag from upstairs."

"I thought you didn't get out to the stores," I said.

"I was only teasing," she said. "Has the Easter Bunny ever let you down?"

Dad came back and Mom passed us each a Mr. Solid and a chocolate egg. Each of the eggs came in their own cardboard box, and through the plastic window we could see our names written in white icing. I opened it up and cracked off the *F*. Mom ruffled my hair. "Sorry the Easter Bunny slept in," she said. "The pills make her sleepy."

That night we sat around the table, all seven of us, stuffing ourselves with turkey. I was grateful that God was being good to us. I hoped he was being good to the Hanrahans too.

★

It stopped snowing overnight and the next day the city got dug out. The plows were loud but the sound I liked the most was the screech of the clothesline. It was cold but sunny, and Mom was in her element.

"It's some day on clothes," she called to Mrs. O'Brien, who was shoveling her back step.

Mrs. O'Brien laughed. "Indeed it is."

Nan spooned some oatmeal into Gord's mouth.

"Did you see his tooth?" I said. "It looks like a Chiclet."

"He's some boy," she said.

Mom came in looking satisfied. "When the roads are clear, I think I'll go get some sleepers for the new baby."

Just then Shelagh came downstairs. Her hand was on her stomach and she was crying. We jumped up, all three of us.

"What's wrong?" said Mom.

Shelagh's voice was a whisper. "Bob broke up with me."

★

Pius said he was going to punch Bob's schnoz in again.

Dad told him he was going to do no such thing.

"His family thinks I'm a slut," said Shelagh. "They want to know how they can be sure the baby is Bob's."

"Well, it'll be pretty obvious if it comes out with a giant nose," I said.

"Finbar!" said Nan. "You of all people should know it's never nice to make fun of people's appearance."

"How dare you bring up my cheek at a time like this," I said.

Mom put her arms around Shelagh. "Things will settle down," she said. "They'll come around."

"And what if they don't?"

"You have us," said Mom. "And we'll always be here for you."

"Hair, hair," I said, wondering if it was *here, here*.

Dad waved a VHS tape in the air. "I think we could all use a laugh."

We gathered around the TV and when *Fawlty Towers* came on, we chuckled because the sign outside the hotel said FARTY TOWELS.

★

Going back to school after a long weekend was always hard, but I managed to arrive at Mr. McGraw's class on time and hungry for taffy.

"Good morning, sir," I said. "I do hope you have a pastel blue on hand."

Mr. McGraw smiled. "I'm sure I do."

Halfway through the class, Damian Clarke passed me a picture of Mikhail Gorbachev. There was an arrow pointing to the port-wine stain on his bald head. Written across the top were the words "Finbar Squires's long-lost dad."

I smiled. "That's funny," I said. "Real funny."

Then I tipped Damian's desk over with him in it.

The upside was Mrs. Muckle had a package of Purity Ginger Snaps on her desk, so even though I had to write "I will control my temper" one hundred times, I had some cookies for energy.

★

After school, Saibal and I took Gord to Fred's Records. We asked Tony to put on The Wiggles' "Big Red Car" and to our surprise, he did. We pushed Gord around the store and Tony sang along. Gord shrieked to the *toot-toot*s and the *chugga-chugga*s, and customers looked at him like he was the cutest thing on earth, which he was. Afterwards we walked to Lar's Fruit Store—but we didn't buy fruit, we bought custard cones, and when Gord tried to hold his, I said, "Look, Saibal. He has dimples where his knuckles should be," and Saibal said, "He's some cute."

On the way back to York Street, we found a pay phone and looked up Bob the Schnoz's number. It wasn't under Schnoz, though. It was under Myrick, which was his last name.

"It's ringing," I said.

"Hello?"

The voice sounded motherly.

"Do you have Robin Hood by the bag?"

"Um . . . yes, I do."

"God almighty, woman! You'd better let him go!"

I hung up.

It was Saibal's turn.

"Hello?"

"Do you have Aunt Jemima by the box?"

The motherly voice turned not-so-motherly.

"Don't call back here again, you little shaggers!"

We doubled over laughing. Gord too.

"That'll teach 'em," I said, though I wasn't sure what.

Saibal opened the phone book. "What's your bully's name, Finbar?"

I grinned. "Damian Clarke. Why?"

He smiled. "You'll see."

He flipped to the *C*s. I scanned the listings and pointed. "That one."

He dialed the number and held the receiver to both our ears.

"Hello?"

It was Damian.

"Oh, hello," said Saibal. "Can I speak to Mrs. Wall, please?"

"Sorry, wrong number."

"How about Mr. Wall?"

"I said wrong number."

"What about Harry Wall? Is he there?"

"No."

"Sally Wall?"

"How many times? You've got the wrong number!"

"I don't understand," said Saibal. "There are no Walls in your house at all?"

"None!"

"That's weird," he said. "What's holding up your roof?"

He slammed the phone down and we burst out laughing.

"Thanks, Saibal," I said. "That made my day."

He clapped me on the shoulder. "Anytime."

We were just leaving the pay phone when a man with a bottle in a brown paper bag staggered toward us. He stopped in front of me and said, "With a face like that, I'd walk backwards."

"Piss off," said Saibal.

"Shut up, wog," said the man.

For once I was speechless.

Saibal grabbed the stroller and almost mowed the man down. "Come on, Finbar."

When we got home, he told Nan what had happened. "You poor little things," she said. She sliced off two huge slabs of her homemade bread and slathered them in partridgeberry jam. Saibal dug right in but I just stared at mine. It was funny how you could know something and not know it at the same time. Like the word *wog*. I hadn't heard it before, but I knew what it meant by the way it was said.

"Saibal?" I said.

"I'm okay," he said. "Eat your bread."

I took a bite.

"I'm okay too," I said, in case he was wondering.

"I know you are, Finbar," he said. "You're hard as nails."

He invited me to his house for supper. Pius pulled me aside before we left. He said I should bring a banana, because banana was good for cooling down hot and spicy curry. Turns out they served Jiggs Dinner. Mr. and Mrs. Sharma were really nice. Out of the blue, because they were doctors, I said, "How much would it be to get this taken off my face?"

Mr. Sharma said he was no expert but he did a dermatology residency once. He said laser surgery was a possibility but he wasn't sure if it was covered by the government. Mrs. Sharma said I was a beautiful boy and I should leave my face alone.

Later, at home, I sat next to Gord's crib. He was already asleep. I watched his breath go in and out, in and out. I hoped he'd never hear the word *wog*. I reached through the slats and stroked his cheek. He'd be beautiful no matter what.

★

It was blowing a gale and the whole house shook. I had trouble falling asleep but eventually I did, and when I woke it was dark and my life had changed.

I couldn't see Pius but I could sense him. He slid one hand behind my lower back and the other onto my shoulder blade. As he pulled me toward him, I knew something bad had happened. I could feel it in the tremble of his hands. In the tremble of his breath. In the tremble in the air around us.

He moved a hand up to the back of my head and pulled me into his cold, bare chest. He'd have spoken if he could but how could he speak the unspeakable?

The wind rattled the window. I imagined myself outside.

When I looked to the heavens, they opened up. Hail pelted my face. I said, "It's okay, God. I'm hard as nails." I stayed in that moment until Pius started rocking. Back and forth. Back and forth. He said, "Oh God, oh God, oh God," and I said, "Nan?" and he made a sound that was a gulp and a sob, and when he said, "No, not Nan," I knew. I wrapped my arms around his waist and said, "But he's just a baby."

★

Pius pulled a blanket around us. "The wind woke Mom, so she decided to check on him. She knew he was gone right away."

I didn't ask how. I didn't want to know.

The paramedics and police were still in the house when Pius took me downstairs. Dad's nose and eyes were red. He was thanking the paramedics. I didn't know what for.

When Dad saw me, his bottom lip shook. "They said it might be cot death."

I said, "Cots don't kill babies."

It was almost May but it felt like December. I shivered in my pajamas. Dad turned up the heat and reached into a laundry basket. He grabbed a shirt that was folded on top, a green plaid flannel, one of his. He helped me into it.

Pius said, "I'm going back up."

"I don't want to go," I said.

Dad sat with me on the couch. He had a hand on my leg. We stared at the coffee table.

After many minutes Dad took my hand. I didn't want to follow him but I did.

Mom was sitting in a rocker by the window. The Humpty Dumpty blanket was in her arms. I assumed Gord was in it.

Nan stood above her. Her eyes were puffy and swollen.

Shelagh was in the corner, rubbing her swollen belly like it was a crystal ball. That's when I started to hate her.

Mom looked up. Her face looked different. It was longer. Like her muscles had stopped working.

"Come here, love," she said.

I felt a growling, deep in my belly. "No."

"Barry," said Dad.

Shelagh reached for me. She had a nerve, the traitor. Having a baby when Gord was gone.

"You," I growled. "You stay away from me."

I felt Pius's hands on my shoulders. "This might be your last chance."

I twisted away, almost knocking him over.

"Barry," he said. "Stop."

"Let him go," said Dad.

A paramedic blocked my way at the front door. "Son—"

My hands formed fists, so I started to punch him. He grabbed my wrists. I wanted to fall into his chest and cry but that would mean someone died, so I kneed him in the groin.

I ran to Bannerman Park and sat on a swing. It was dark and cold and the wind howled. I hoped Gord wasn't scared of the rattling at his window. I sat till the sun came up. Dad's shirt was a hug. My stomach growled. Gord would be up soon. I'd make him his oatmeal, just like usual. I sat some more. I wondered why Pius had been hugging me while I was trying to sleep. Must have been a dream. Kids passed in the distance, schoolbags on their backs. Shit. Gord's oatmeal. Never mind. Nan would have made it by now. She'd have sprinkled it with cinnamon. He'd have liked that.

After a while, I walked to school. Everyone stared.

"Barry," said Thomas Budgell. "What are you wearing?"

I looked down. My pants had Spiderman on them. Like they were pajamas or something.

I went to Mr. McGraw's class. I remembered some kind of deal. A reward if I was good. I took my seat. When Mr. McGraw saw me, he said, "Barry, can I talk to you outside?" It was a familiar feeling, being pulled out of class. I said, "Did I do something bad?" And he said, "Barry, I'm so sorry." My hands formed fists, so I started to punch him. He grabbed my wrists and I fell into his chest. He put his arms around me but I don't know for how long because the world wasn't spinning properly, not since I'd had that bad dream about Gord dying.

★

Dad took me home. He said, "Gord's at the funeral home."

They cried all day long. The bastards. They didn't *have* to believe it. No one was forcing them.

I went to the war memorial. When Saibal saw me, he put his head in his hands.

I stroked his hair. "Don't cry. It didn't really happen."

He looked up. "It didn't?"

I pulled my hand up my sleeve and wiped his tears.

"Of course it didn't."

He wanted to believe me, so I said, "Come on. I'll show you."

The house was busy with visitors.

"That's weird," I said. "There must be some kind of celebration."

I snuck inside. A moment later I was pushing the stroller toward Saibal.

"Gord is *so* glad to be out of there," I said. "Houseguests make such a fuss over him."

Saibal looked at the stroller.

Then he looked at me.

"Jesus, Finbar. You left his coat wide open."

My eyes filled with tears.

He bent down and zipped up the imaginary zipper.

"Let's take him up Signal Hill," he said.

Passersby stared as we made our way up.

"Your turn, Saibal," I said. "He's getting heavy."

Saibal took over. "You're some fat, Gord. You're like a tub of lard."

At the top of the hill, Saibal tightened Gord's seatbelt. "You ready, Gord?"

I ran ahead and braced myself. "Okay, Saibal. Let him go!"

The stroller raced toward me.

I could see him.

Plain as day.

Gummy smile.

Wisps of hair blowing in the wind.

Big blue eyes staring at me.

I caught him around the waist.

"I gotcha, Gord. I gotcha."

I fell on my knees and draped my arms over the empty stroller.

Saibal draped his arms over mine.

"What are we going to do, Saibal?"

"I don't know, Finbar."

★

We sat cross-legged on the sidewalk.

"I don't want Shelagh's baby to have the stroller."

Saibal looked around. "We could throw it in Dead-man's Pond."

We pushed it through the bushes and to the water's edge. Saibal took one end and I took the other.

"One, two, three."

One big splash and it was gone.

We walked back home. All around us the world ticked along. People went about their business and I thought, "Don't they know? A baby died today."

Saibal hugged everyone in my family, even Shelagh. Mom hugged him the longest. She said, "Gord loved you. Did you know that?" and all he could do was nod. The kitchen was full of food brought by neighbors. I wasn't hungry but Nan said I had to eat. Saibal and I sat in the kitchen eating beef stew. When Shelagh came in, I dropped my spoon. Saibal followed me to my room.

"I hate her," I said.

He nodded. "I know."

We played Go Fish until it was time for him to leave.

Before he left I asked him to keep going to the war memorial.

"I don't want things to change," I said, even though everything had.

"I'll be there every day," he said. "Promise."

★

I went to sleep.

When I woke it was still dark.

I went to Gord's room.

I sat on the floor and put my hand between the slats.

I moved my hand around the empty space.

Then I went to my parents' room and climbed between them. They wrapped their arms around me. I prayed in my head. *Please, God, tell them to tell me it'll be okay.* They didn't pass on his message. Maybe they didn't believe it. Or maybe God never told them in the first place. Maybe he'd failed me again.

★

Nan was a machine. Cooking, cleaning, making and taking calls. I walked past the bathroom. She was on her hands and knees. Shelagh passed by too. She said, "Scrubbing that toilet won't bring him back," and I said, "Shut up, Shelagh," not because I disagreed but because I hated her.

★

For the next few days, blood and breath ran through our bodies but we were barely alive. We were half dead. Maybe three-quarters. A big fat chunk of us was missing. A ginormous tub of lard.

I saw Dad sitting on his bed, his wristwatch in his hand. He said, "I wonder what time he died."

It was a weird thing to wonder. What did it matter?

"What time was he born?" I asked.

My father was as surprised by my question as I'd been by his.

"2:33 a.m.," he said. "He was a chubby little thing. Thighs like a speed skater." Dad smiled just a bit. He strapped his watch around his wrist. "I miss him, Barry."

"I know," I said. "Me too."

★

Saibal was at the war memorial with two birch beers.

"What do you want to do today?" he asked.

"I want to kick the shit out of the floor."

We went to the nursing home. They all knew. It was in the paper. They didn't say much. I got a few sorrys, and a hug from Buster and Edie, and that was it. I appreci-ated that. I wasn't there to talk.

We went to the Last Chance Saloon. We were so loud, we drew a crowd. The songs were lively—"Squid Jiggin' Ground," "Aunt Martha's Sheep," "Feller from Fortune" . . . When I pictured the Humpty Dumpty blanket, I danced harder. When I pictured Gord dead, I sang louder.

Before I left, Buster asked when the funeral was. I said, "Don't know. Don't care." He opened his mouth to say something, then closed it. As I walked out the door he told me to take care and I said, "Will do."

CHAPTER EIGHT

There was a visitation at the funeral home. I went to the
Harbour Light Centre instead. Uneven Steven told me
that when he was little, his sister died. She was born with
a disease and died when she was two.

"Did you see her after she died?" I asked.

"Yes," he said. "I held her."

"I didn't hold Gord. If he's an angel, he's probably mad."

"Gord? Mad?" he said.

I smiled. Gord was the happiest baby on earth.

We spent the rest of the day playing cards around the
big kitchen table. The men talked about their lives. They
were tough and broken and soft and hard, and they said
they wouldn't be defined by their pasts, and I hoped I'd

always be defined by Gord because if I wasn't, he might get forgotten.

*

"I'm not going."

I said it ten million times.

Nan threw her hands up in the air. "We can't force him. What are we going to do? Tie him to the car?"

"Don't be an arsehole, Barry," said Pius.

Mom and Dad were too tired to argue.

Shelagh rubbed her belly. "Come on, Barry. You have to go."

I picked up a vase of flowers and threw them against the wall.

"Fuck you."

I wanted Mom to call me Fin-bear, but she stared at the flowers. "Those were from the O'Briens."

"Clean that up, Barry," said Dad.

Then they left.

I sat in the front window and stared out at York Street. A car pulled up. Saibal got out. He was wearing a suit. He waved to me. "You coming?" I shook my head. He stared at me. I stared at him. He got back in his car and drove away.

I went to Caines. Boo said, "How are you doing, Barry?"

"I'd like a sour key, please."

"Here ya go," he said. "On the house."

I wandered around downtown sucking on it.

I was at the intersection of Duckworth and Prescott when I heard the *beep-beep-beep* of a car horn. I turned around. The One Step Closer to God minibus was careening toward me.

"God almighty!" I yelled.

The bus jumped the curb and came to a stop near my foot. The door opened.

"Quick," yelled Buster. "Get in!"

I hopped on board and took a seat next to Edie.

"I didn't know you could drive a bus," I said.

He laughed. "I can't."

"Where are we going?" I asked.

"Where do you think?" said Edie.

I stood up. "I'm not going."

Buster put his foot on the gas. "Oh yes, you are."

I fell back into my seat.

"The church is full," said Edie. "But it feels empty without you."

I said out loud what I'd been thinking all day. "I don't want to see the coffin."

Buster and Edie exchanged a look through the rear-view mirror.

Edie took my hand. "There's a big picture of Gord on a table at the front of the church," she said. "He's wearing a pair of sleepers with monkeys on them."

"He's smiling at the camera," said Buster. "His tongue is stuck out and there's drool dribbling down his chin."

"You focus on that, Barry," said Edie. "Think of it as a celebration of his life."

I didn't feel like celebrating but I did feel like remembering.

"Okay," I said.

Edie took my hand and I relaxed as much as I could in a speeding bus.

★

Heads turned as I walked in. Mom and Dad moved apart so I could sit between them. They each took a hand and gave it a squeeze. I was the baby now but I didn't want to be.

Father O'Flaherty shot me a dirty look, which I thought was pretty outrageous considering the circumstances. I immediately tuned him out. I focused on the photo of Gord in his monkey pajamas. I pictured how happy Gord was when I pretended to dump him in the harbor. Then I heard Pius's voice. He was up at the altar. He talked about how smart Gord was. And how funny and cute. I heard the rustle of paper and when I looked up, he smiled and said, "I asked friends and neighbors to share their memories." Boo from Caines said Gord was his favorite customer. Tony from Fred's said Gord lit up the whole store. Mrs. O'Brien said she loved the sound of Gord's laugh ringing from our open window to hers.

I looked back at the photo.

My heart was full but it felt empty without him.

★

Father O'Flaherty shook our hands. When it was my turn, I said, "Your oral presentation skills need work."

He said, "This anger will pass, my son."

Pius came over and pulled me outside. He spread his arms apart and said, "Punch me."

I took a swing. He'd tensed but I managed to knock some wind out of him.

He caught his breath. "Better?"

I nodded.

He spread his arms apart again. I walked into them.

He said, "We'll get through this," and I almost believed him.

★

Back at the house Nan told Mrs. O'Brien that they think Gord died of SIDS.

"Sid's what?" I asked.

Nan added three sugars to my tea. "Sudden Infant Death Syndrome."

I poured my tea down the sink.

Saibal and his parents came to give their condolences. They were two of the many people who came to visit. It felt like a party but it was far from it. Saibal came to my room and we played Operation. I kept hitting the sides but Saibal had a steady hand.

"You have the hands of a surgeon," I said.

Saibal extracted the broken heart. "Runs in the family," he said.

I tried for the funny bone. *BZZZZZZ.*

"You, on the other hand," said Saibal, "have the hands of a sturgeon."

I laughed because sturgeons don't have hands.

"Saibal?" I said. "Can you get your mom and dad?"

A moment later they were at the end of my bed. I addressed my first question to his mother.

"Tell me," I said. "How in God's name can a baby's heart stop for no reason?"

She opened her mouth but nothing came out.

"You don't know?" I said. "Some heart doctor you are."

"And what about this SIDS business?" I said to his father. "Sounds like a load of old poppycock to me."

Saibal's mom spoke softly. "Being angry is normal—"

"I'm not fucking angry," I said.

Saibal's dad stood up. "We'll give you a few minutes to calm down."

When they left, I kicked the Operation game to the floor. "Some help they were."

Saibal took another game off my shelf. "Battleship?"

"Okay."

After I sunk his battleship, I said, "Can you go get your parents again?"

A few moments later they were back.

Saibal's dad spoke first. "Your parents are happy for us to answer any questions you might have."

"I only have one," I said.

He nodded. "Go on."

My voice broke when I said it.

"Why?"

★

Sometimes bad things happen to good people. That's what they said. It wasn't a very satisfying answer but then they explained SIDS. They said it's the sudden, unexplained death of a child under the age of one. It's unpredictable and unpreventable. Researchers are working to understand it. I listened real hard. The army men in my head stood at attention. I understood everything but it was hard to take. I didn't want it to be true. When they were done, I said sorry for earlier. They said I was going to have lots of ups and downs, and that grieving is complicated. They invited me for supper the following evening and I said, "Let me know if you're making curry so I can bring a banana." It felt weird to laugh but I figured it was just one little up in a million downs.

★

We sat around the table, just the six of us. Dad wanted to check in, see how we were doing. The visitors were gone and the house was so quiet I could hear the refrigerator hum. Nan opened a tin of shortbread cookies from Mrs. Hanrahan. Shelagh took one and spoke to her belly. "Hope you like butter, little one," she said. "Shortbread's my favorite."

"No one cares about your stupid baby," I said.

"Finbar," said Nan. "That's not fair."

"You know what else isn't fair?" I said.

Shelagh stood up. "I'm going to bed."

"Please stay," said Mom.

Pius took a pile of sympathy cards off the kitchen counter.

"Come on," he said. "Let's have a look through these. Together."

Mom smiled at him. "My sweet sixteen."

She hadn't used the nickname in months. Pius blushed at the sound of it.

Shelagh sat back down.

Dad opened the first one. "This one is from"—he squinted at the signature—"the Fizzards? Who in God's name are they?"

Nan laughed. "No idea."

"Wait now," said Mom. "The Fizzards live out on Barnes Road. Dennis Fizzard is Aunt Jacinta's brother-in-law."

"Oh yes," said Nan. "Now aren't they the ones that always had a cow tied up in their front yard?"

"A cow?" said Pius. "No way."

"Yes way," said Dad. "And on Christmas Eve in '82— or was it '83?—the cow escaped and ran over the crowds coming out of midnight mass."

"Are you serious?" said Shelagh.

"Oh yes," said Mom. "Father Molloy sprained his ankle that night."

"Too bad he didn't end up in a full body cast," I said.

Mom patted my hand. "Now, now, Fin-bear."

The next card made everyone cry. It was from a Mrs. Down in Harbour Grace.

"Who's Mrs. Down?" asked Dad.

Mom looked up from the card. "She lost a baby to SIDS. Emily Louise. She was eleven weeks old."

So it was a real thing. Cots *did* kill babies.

Dad picked up the envelope. He traced the curly writing with his finger like it was from a long lost friend.

Some of the cards were Hallmark but even the flimsy and cheap ones meant something.

That night I heard Mom wailing from her bedroom.

At two in the morning I went to the bathroom and heard a noise outside. I looked out the window and saw Nan sweeping the sidewalk outside our house.

Grief was complicated.

★

A week later Dad went back to work. He wore his watch around his wrist. It seemed to weigh him down on one side. He put clocks in every room. All day long, it was a bloody cacophony of ticks and tocks. "Every moment counts," he said. Mom went back in her room. I rarely saw her. Every now and then I'd knock on her door and sometimes she'd say, "Come in." I'd open the window and say, "It's some day on clothes," but she'd just put her arms out and I'd climb into them. We'd lie there staring at the popcorn ceiling, neither of us saying a word. When I'd leave, she'd say, "Shut the window, Barry."

★

I dropped a pencil in class once. Damian Clarke picked it up and said, "Here ya go, buddy," so I stabbed him with it.

Mrs. Muckle said, "What are we going to do with you, Barry?"

I said I didn't know.

★

Sometimes, at supper, Nan pulled Gord's high chair to the table but it slid across the floor too quickly.

The weight of him, it was everything.

★

I dreamt of Mom by the window, a blanket in her lap. I'd walk toward her but then I'd wake. One night I stayed dreaming. I peeled the blanket back. It was a Cabbage Patch Kid. My head was sweaty and my throat hurt from the scream. Pius said, "You okay, Barry?" I said, "Ever wish it would all go away?" and he said, "Every day."

★

Shelagh got fatter and fatter. If I had a magic wand, I'd make it stop.

★

The days and weeks melted into each other. Someone set fire to them and watched them burn. I don't know who. Maybe it was God. May became June. The weather was warming up and school was coming to an end. People asked me how I was but I had no idea. I should have recorded myself so I could watch it back. Did I go to school every day? I must have. Would I pass eighth grade and move on to high school? Who knew? The only thing I knew was that Gord was still dead and time was moving further away from his ever existing.

★

Saibal sat at the war memorial in a T-shirt and jeans. "Some warm out, isn't it?"

I supposed it was for Newfoundland. There was a chill in the air, but at least the sun was out.

"Practically tropical," I said.

"Gord would have liked summer," he said.

I stretched out on the grass.

"Sometimes I watch the time change on my alarm clock. The second hand is lucky. It gets to *tick-tick-tick*, but the minute hand has to just sit there, watching time pass and waiting to move forward."

Saibal sat next to me. He put a blade of grass between his thumbs and blew. It made a whistling sound. I sat up.

"How did you do that?"

He picked me a blade and showed me how. It worked on my first blow.

We experimented with the way we held the grass to make different notes. We tried to play "Three Blind Mice." It sounded decent.

"Saibal?" I said.

"Yeah?"

"Sometimes . . . I think I need to see your mom. As a patient. Because my heart pains all the time."

"Maybe I could borrow her paddle thingies," he said, "and shock your heart back to its old self."

"Nah," I said. "You might accidentally kill me. Then where would we be?"

"True. Your parents can't go through that again."

We went to Caines and listened to Boo tell ghost stories. Some were really spooky. Gruesome even. But I wasn't scared. The scariest thing in the world had already happened.

Afterwards, Saibal and I walked out to the Battery. We sat overlooking the Narrows and watched a tour boat putter toward open water.

I said, "You went all the way out to King William Estates to get your bank card and I didn't even say thanks."

"That's okay."

"You prank-called Damian Clarke too. On my behalf. I should have prank-called Freddie Fudge but I didn't."

"It's okay, Finbar."

"No, it's not," I said. "I took you for granted."

I pulled a clump of grass out of the earth. "I took Gord for granted too."

Saibal made his hand into a fist. For a second I thought he was going to punch me, but he ran his fingers along his knuckles. "Remember Gord's dimples?" he said. "Ten little dents where his knuckles should be. You always seemed to notice the little things."

My eyes filled with tears.

"My heart's hurting again, Saibal."

He pushed me over and straddled my waist. "Clear!"

He hit my chest with an imaginary defibrillator and

I jolted with the almighty shock. I stared into the sky and said, "Look, Saibal. A pair of boobs." He lay beside me. "An elephant too." The clouds moved by slowly just for us. We watched them while my heart recovered.

★

I sat in the front window. Mrs. Inkpen's dog, Labatt, greeted her by stealing one of her nursing shoes. Mr. O'Brien went straight to his bedroom and changed from his mechanic coveralls to his Snoopy pajama bottoms. Mr. Power came home and went straight to his wife for a kiss. Funny thing was, Gord was still dead. Our car puttered up and pulled over. I ran to the door. Dad put his arms around me and ruffled my hair. He said I was a grand boy and we should go out for a plate of chips, so that's just what we did.

★

Usually a whiff of June would stir up the excitement of summer, but not even a custard cone from Lar's could revive the butterflies that lay dead in my belly. The ice cream was sweet and cool and velvety smooth, but there was no little tongue leaning in for a lick, so I was left with a bad taste in my mouth.

June in Newfoundland meant going out in shorts and T-shirts and hoping the weather got the point. I wore Pius's old soccer shorts and AC/DC shirt almost every day because it made me feel like he was near, though why I wanted that I didn't know.

Saibal and I were glued at the hip. One day we got the bus to the Avalon Mall. We tried to sneak into a movie but got kicked out. The security guard called us Crockett and Tubbs. I said, "I'm not fat." The security guard said I needed to brush up on *Miami Vice*.

On the bus home, Saibal said, "Tubbs is black. Crockett's the white one. He wears shoes with no socks."

"That's a blister waiting to happen," I said.

We stopped in to Mary Brown's on the way home for a two-piece and taters. I held up my drumstick and said, "Mary Brown's—she's got the best legs in town."

Saibal smiled. "Open twenty-four hours a day!"

We took a handful of straws and blew the wrappers off. One landed on a high chair.

That was what June was like. Even the ups felt like downs.

★

On the last day of school I was the first to arrive at Mr. McGraw's class.

He took off his blazer and hung it on the back of his chair. "Well, well," he said. "I don't believe it."

"I went to Bannerman Park at six," I said. "I sat on a swing till my arse hurt."

He sat at his desk.

"Whenever I wake up now I can't get back to sleep," I said. "Because Gord is the first thing that pops into my mind. I mean, I can't just close my eyes and forget about him, can I? That wouldn't be very nice."

"Finbar," said Mr. McGraw. "Have you thought about talking to someone?"

I frowned. "I'm talking to you, aren't I?"

He smiled. "I suppose you are."

I scraped my nail on the wooden desk. "I like you, Mr. McGraw. Ditching your class wasn't about you. It was about me. It was about me being a puzzle piece with the ends all bashed up. I'll always stick out this way and that. First it was my face and now it's Gord. I feel like everyone's always looking at me. I hate it. It makes me feel really unconscious."

"I think you mean *self*-conscious," he said.

I smiled. "If you like."

I scraped a splinter out of the wood. I held it between my thumb and forefinger. It was thick on one end and pointy at the other, like a miniature sword. It'd be perfect for poking the likes of Damian Clarke and Thomas Budgell. It might even draw blood.

"I like it in the principal's office," I said. "I have my own desk there and the only person to bother me is Mrs. Muckle."

Mr. McGraw followed my eyes to the clock on the wall. Four minutes to the bell.

"Come here, Barry," he said.

I went to the front of the room. Mr. McGraw pulled open his desk drawer.

"Help yourself."

I chose a pastel blue.

"Tell Mrs. Muckle I sent you," he said. "You can make up the reason why."

I passed him my miniature sword. "I'll miss you, sir."

He took the sword and smiled. "I'll miss you too."

★

I waited for two minutes past the bell before waltzing into her office.

"Oh, for goodness sake, Barry," said Mrs. Muckle. "What now?"

"It wasn't my fault," I said, laying my schoolbag next

to my desk. "Thomas Budgell was being an arsehole, so I stabbed him with a miniature sword."

Her eyes widened. "With a what?"

I sat down. "Don't worry. It only drew two drops of blood. Three, tops."

She leaned back in her chair. "What are we going to do with you, Barry?"

"Nothing," I said. "It's the last day of school. I'll be out of your hair soon and you can forget all about me."

"Impossible," she said. "How do you forget the unforgettable?"

"You don't," I said. "Especially when the unforgettable is bad like me. Good things, though, you get scared of losing. Like what if they fade and you forget them forever?"

She came out from around her desk and crouched before me.

"It's the bad things that fade over time, Barry. I promise. You'll never forget Gord, and I'll never forget you."

I focused on her fantabulous slut shoes to keep my heart from aching.

"When I think of him," I said, "I think of that night. It ruins my memories."

"It won't always be that way," she said. "You just need to give it time."

She gave me a sheet of lined paper and a pen.

"I want three memories," she said. "The very best of all."

I wrote them quickly and with a smile on my face.

1. Watching him sleep.
2. Pretending to dump him in the harbor.
3. That time Saibal and me let him roll down Signal Hill Road.

"Interesting," said Mrs. Muckle. "Why these?"

"The first one was when I was the happiest, the second one was when Gord was happiest, and the third one includes Saibal."

Mrs. Muckle laughed. "Gord was happiest when he thought he was being dumped in the harbor?"

I smiled to think of it. "He shrieked his friggin' head off."

★

When I got home, Nan gave me a lassy bun and a cup of tea.

I looked to the ceiling. "What was that?"

"What was what?" she said.

"That noise," I said. "Sounds like someone's moving furniture."

Nan's voice went up an octave. "I didn't hear anything."

She was a terrible liar.

I pictured the layout of the house and ran upstairs.

"Get your grubby hands off Gord's stuff or by da Jesus, I'll knock you into next week."

Shelagh took a step back. "We just thought if we rearranged it, it would—"

"It would what?" I said. "Make us forget all about Gord so we can concentrate on your stupid kid?"

Shelagh started to cry. "You think this is easy for me?"

Nan appeared in the doorway. "Finbar, calm down."

"This is Gord's room!" I yelled.

Mom pulled the Humpty Dumpty blanket off the crib rail and moved to the chair by the window. Suddenly the wind, it was blowing a gale. The house was dark and our whole life changed. It was never going to go away, that feeling. That feeling of being robbed. We stood there, all four of us, wondering how we'd get through.

Mom reached her hand out to me. I went to her and took it. I imagined myself outside. Hail pelted my face. I said, "Help me, God. It hurts."

Mom gave my hand a squeeze. I squeezed back.

"Maybe," I said, "the chair would be better by the door. And the crib, we could put that against the wall near the window."

A moment later we set about moving the furniture. I opened the window, let the bad memories out.

Afterwards, Shelagh touched my arm. "Thanks, Barry."

I pulled away. "I didn't do it for you. I did it for Mom."

I did it for Gord too.

The wind had no business in his room.

CHAPTER NINE

One morning in mid-July, I sat on Uneven Steven's cardboard and said, "If Shelagh's baby doesn't come out dead, I might kill it myself."

"Is that so?" he said.

I passed him one of Nan's partridgeberry muffins.

"I hope it's born with a port-wine stain all over its body."

He broke the muffin in two and offered me the top half.

"Have you ever noticed how ugly Shelagh is?" I said. "I don't know why anyone would want to have sex with her."

I smashed the muffin in my fist.

"She thinks her baby is the second coming of Jesus. She rubs her big, fat belly like it's something special. Mom and Dad do too. When they talk about the baby, they look happy, even though they're supposed to be sad. Wait till they see the hideous little gremlin that claws its way out of Shelagh's hoo-ha. That'll wipe the smile off their faces, the bastards."

I killed a few ants with the heel of my sneaker.

Steven licked a crumb off his bottom lip. "Anything else you'd like to get off your ol' George Best?"

I stood up. "No," I said. "I think that's it."

"Have a nice day, Squire."

"You too, Steven."

★

I walked toward the war memorial, wishing the sunshine was mist. I wanted to feel alive in a good way, not from the anger that pulsed through my veins.

"Saibal," I said. "I need your help."

He didn't ask with what, he just followed me back to the house. When no one was looking, we took the high chair.

"Deadman's Pond," I said.

Saibal nodded. "Understood."

We lugged it up Signal Hill Road. When we got to the pond, we collapsed from exhaustion.

"Jesus, Mary, and Joseph," said Saibal.

"And all the saints in heaven," I added.

The high chair was on its side. On the underside of the tray there was some dried oatmeal. I scraped it with my fingernail. It didn't budge.

"I wish your parents were here," I said. "I want to ask them a question."

"Ask me," said Saibal. "I'm smart."

I pointed to the tray. "Is Gord's DNA on this?"

Saibal squinted at the crusty oatmeal. "I would say so."

I examined the bottom of the tray. There was Gord crud everywhere.

"We don't have to throw it in Deadman's Pond," said Saibal.

"We don't?"

He shook his head. "Want to take it back home?"

"You don't mind?"

Saibal stood up and swept some loose grass off his shorts. "Let's go."

On the way back down the hill, I paused. "Wait. What if, before Shelagh's little monster arrives, they clean the high chair from top to bottom? What if they wash Gord away?"

Saibal had a look underneath. "From those crevices? Not even your nan could clean them out."

When we got home, Nan caught us with the high chair but turned a blind eye.

"Now," she said. "Who wants a nice cup of tea?"

She put the kettle on and showed us an invitation she'd received in the mail.

"I couldn't believe my eyes," she said. "The return address said Government House!"

Saibal and I smiled at each other.

"I'm impressed," said Saibal. "You've really got to be someone to get an invitation to the garden party."

"And you're something else," I said.

Nan smiled. "I suppose I am."

She topped up our tea from the pot.

"Nan?" I said. "Do you think I can come too?"

"I don't see why not," she said.

"You'll get to meet the lieutenant governor," said Saibal.

But I didn't care about that. I wanted to see Big Gord again.

★

Dad came home from work just before lunchtime.

"I took the afternoon off," he said. "Let's head out to Topsail Beach."

"The beach?" said Mom.

Dad pointed at his watch. "It's eleven forty-five. If we leave in fifteen, we'll be there by twelve thirty."

He turned to Nan. "Do you think you can throw a picnic together for us?"

"I certainly can," said Nan.

"What do you mean *for us*?" I asked. "Isn't Nan coming too?"

"Of course not. Where would she sit?" said Pius. "On the roof?"

"Maybe Shelagh can stay home," I suggested. "And Nan can come instead."

"Now, Barry," said Nan.

Mom looked around the kitchen. "I was going to wash the floors today."

Pius pulled a cooler out of the cupboard on the back porch. "You can wash the floors tomorrow."

"Don't worry," said Nan. "I'll take care of the floors."

"Can we stop for ice cream?" asked Shelagh.

"Shut up, you fat pig," I said.

"Barry," said Dad. "Enough."

He went to Mom, took her hand. "It'll be a grand day, I promise."

Nan waved from the window as we piled into the car. I refused to sit near Shelagh. Dad pulled me aside and told me to give it a rest. Pius overheard and said he didn't mind, he'd sit in the middle. He'd been pretty nice since Gord died, but I'd rather he was mean.

We headed out on Portugal Cove Road. We drove for a long time. Every now and then we'd round a bend and see the ocean. Then it would disappear again.

"I feel sick," said Shelagh.

We stopped at a convenience store with a big ice-cream cone outside. Shelagh ordered a double scoop.

"I thought you were sick," I said.

"Shut up, Barry."

She looked like the side of a house. I hoped she stuffed her face till she blew up.

I had a single scoop. Neapolitan. I wanted to give Gord a lick.

We ate our ice cream at a picnic table outside the store.

Pius had his hand on Shelagh's stomach.

"Holy shit," he said between licks. "It's kicking up a storm."

Well, whoop-dee-bloody-do.

Mom didn't have an ice cream but took licks off Dad's orange-pineapple.

"You should have got your own," he said.

She laughed. "I wasn't in the mood but I am now."

He leaned over and kissed her cheek. "This fresh air has done you good."

He went inside and got her a cone of her own.

We drove a while longer and turned down Topsail Beach Road.

"Isn't it grand?" said Mom.

The beach was dotted with people enjoying the sun. We unloaded the car and joined them. Dad told me to hold Shelagh's hand as she navigated the uneven terrain but I pretended not to hear. Pius helped her instead.

Mom and Dad spread two blankets out over the big beach rocks. I waited for Shelagh to settle her fat arse on one so I could choose the other. She sprawled across both. I sat blanket-less a few feet away.

Pius went for a walk. I watched him get smaller in the distance. Beachgoers waded into the ocean, waist high. It was too rough to venture out farther. The waves had all the power of Gord, whooshing in a way that made me breathe slower. In, out, in, out. I imagined his little chest rising and falling. I imagined him in my arms. It would have been his first time at the beach. The breeze would have lifted up his little wisps of hair, like a gentle wind through a field of grass.

My heart pained.

It would always hurt to do something new without Gord.

The problem was, it would always hurt to do something old too.

Like hanging stockings at Christmas.

Gord's was red with a toy soldier on it.

Grief was more than just complicated.

It was a trap.

"I'm going for a walk," I said.

"Be careful," said Mom.

She didn't want me to get swept out to sea. That happens sometimes.

On the shoreline I saw a condom. I'd tell Saibal about it later.

I walked till Mom and Dad were dots. Shelagh would look like a beached whale no matter how far I roamed.

Pius was up ahead skipping stones.

There were tears streaming down his face. Trillions of them.

I picked up a stone. It was flat and shiny and smooth.

"I bet I can skip this six times," I said.

"Bet you can't," he said.

I placed the stone along my pointer finger and secured it with my thumb. I pulled my arm back, cocked my wrist, and released. The stone landed in the water with a plunk.

Pius passed me another one. "Try again, dumbass."

★

We sat around the cooler eating bologna sandwiches.

"Nan must have caught one last night," I said.

"Fierce creatures," said Pius. "They'd bite the hand right off ya."

Our laughter rang from Topsail Beach to Signal Hill. It went into the sky and under the waves. Seabirds celebrated and marine life rejoiced. It danced on the wind in a tumbling whirl. It bounced off the cliffs and zoomed through the universe and then it came back to us, an echo lined with a sweet baby belly laugh.

★

The day came to an end. Ten to five by Dad's watch.

Pius sat in the middle on the way home. Shelagh was still a fat pig, boomerang laughter or not.

★

That night, there was a ruckus.

I sat up in bed. "What's happening?"

Pius was pulling a hoodie over his bare chest. "It's Shelagh. They're taking her to the hospital."

"Oh," I said. "Is that all?"

"Don't be an arsehole, Barry. It's too early. She's only seven months pregnant."

I put my head down and nestled back under my covers. So the baby would be premature. So what? At least it'd be alive.

The minute hand moved slowly on my alarm clock. The second hand mocked it with its *tick-tick-tick*. "Hang in there, buddy," I said. Being patient was hard.

Pius came back forty minutes later. "Dad just called. It was a false alarm. The baby's not coming just yet."

I didn't answer because I was pretending to be asleep.

When I heard Pius snoring, I reached over and pulled the batteries out of my alarm clock. "It's okay, buddy," I whispered. "You can rest now."

★

The next morning I went to Gord's room. His newborn clothes had been freshly laundered. I reached into his dresser and took the monkey sleepers sized 0–3 months. I hid them in the rafters in the basement.

★

I told everyone at the nursing home about the false alarm. Edie said one of her labors lasted seventy-two hours. She called the kid Trouble. I wondered what Shelagh would name her kid. Probably Shitty McShithead or Ugly McUggface.

Buster said I seemed tense, so we danced extra hard and extra long. Saibal taught us a style of Indian dance called bhangra. We bounced our shoulders a lot and raised our hands to the sky. He admitted he didn't know what he was doing, so he sang "The Night Pat Murphy Died" in his Indian accent to add some authenticity.

Afterwards Buster said, "Guess what?" and when I said, "What?" he took out his teeth.

I laughed till I cried.

Edie gave me a medal of Saint Elizabeth. She told me to give it to my mother. I wondered if Saint Elizabeth was the patron saint of dead babies. I looked at the embossed woman on the silver medal and whispered, "Fuck you, Liz." I put it in my pocket and wondered if I'd go to hell.

★

A week later it was the day of the garden party. Nan was all done up like a stick of gum. She had rouge on her cheeks and a hat on her head. Mom made me wear a shirt with buttons and slacks, not jeans. As we walked out the door, she said, "Behave yourself, Fin-bear."

We walked up Cochrane Street. When we reached the top, we could see it: Government House. Nan linked her arm through mine. "Look at all the people," she said. The grounds were full and from where we stood, we could hear the murmur of conversation and the faint sound of the CLB Band.

We crossed Military Road and made our way to the entrance. The gravel path crunched beneath our feet. Nan looked nervous as we joined the party of finely dressed guests.

"Can I go explore?" I said.

Nan nodded. "Be good."

"Good's my middle name," I said.

"I thought it was Turlough," said a voice.

I turned around. Big Gord looked smart in a pinstriped suit. He introduced Nan to the lieutenant governor. Nan curtsied. We ate triangle sandwiches. The CLB Band was playing "Fight the Good Fight." Nan chatted with an army man in a wheelchair. It was hot and I was getting bored. Big Gord nodded to two plastic chairs under a tree. "Let's take a load off." A server came by and offered us lemonade. Big Gord clinked his glass against mine. "Here's to looking up your kilt."

"Up yours too," I said.

He took a long sip. "Ahhh."

I could tell by his face the lemonade was sour.

I took a sip. "Ahhh."

A newspaper man took our picture.

"We might make it into the *Telegram*," said Big Gord.

"My name was in the paper once," I said. "Right after 'leaving to mourn.'"

Big Gord nodded. "I saw that."

"I have a Gord-sized hole now," I said.

He took another sip of his drink.

I did too.

He pointed to a man with medals on his blazer.

"Ralph Fardy," he said. "One hundred and one."

"He's lucky he got to get old," I said.

"Indeed," said Big Gord.

"I've got a medal too," I said.

I took Saint Elizabeth out of my pocket. "I was supposed to give this to my mother."

"Little things can bring great comfort," said Big Gord.

The band played "The St. John's Waltz." Big Gord tapped his foot.

I tapped my foot too.

"This is the kind of song that fills you up," he said.

I didn't ask with what. I knew what it was and it didn't have a name. It was a mixture of feelings that could make you laugh and cry.

I saw Nan near the band. She was swaying to the music in her big hat. I hoped she lived to one hundred and one.

I pictured Dad's wristwatch marking time with its *click-click-click*s. A steady rhythm no matter how time flies.

The song was coming to an end. Big Gord sang about a world of romance and not missing a chance to be dancin' the St. John's Waltz. And his voice, it filled up a spot in my Gord-sized hole.

★

Father O'Flaherty made an appearance before the end of the garden party. He stood in front of the CLB Band and said he had an announcement. There was to be a talent contest on the night of the St. John's Regatta. He said the winner would be picked by audience vote and the prize was six hundred dollars.

"I hope the Full Tilt Dancers can count on your support," he said. "The prize money will go toward new flooring, of which we're in desperate need."

The audience nodded and clapped.

I asked Nan if she could make her way home alone. When she said yes, I ran like the dickens to the nursing home.

★

"Six hundred dollars?" said Buster. "Where do we sign up?"

"We could get a new sound system!" said Edie.

"We could buy tap shoes for all!" said Buster.

I cleared my throat.

"I have a different idea."

It was weird to see their faces light up at the mention of SIDS. But six hundred dollars toward research was something to smile about.

I called Saibal when I got home. "You'd better make up some more bhangra moves," I said. "We've got a dance to choreograph."

When I hung up the phone, I went to find Mom. She was in Gord's room. I reached into my pocket and pulled out the medal.

"Saint Liz," I said.

Mom's eyes crinkled when she laughed. "Oh, Barry."

Big Gord was right. Little things did bring comfort.

★

We only had a week, so we practiced every day. Uneven Steven came because he said he had a lot of expertise in the area. He even brought two fellas from the Harbour Light Centre—one played guitar and one played accordion. We decided on Great Big Sea's "Goin' Up" because it was super lively but not too fast. Our choreography was very unique. Wheelchairs, walkers, canes, and a piece of plywood all played a part. (The plywood was for my solo.) Saibal made up some more bhangra moves, which added an element of the exotic.

On the day before the regatta, Uneven Steven brought in a VHS tape. He wanted to inspire us with a montage of his moves from back in the day. I was curious as to what kind of video proof he could have for what was surely a fictitious life. We sat around a small TV and watched as he popped in the tape and pressed Play. Our jaws dropped as a string of musical clips came to life on the screen. We watched as Steven performed onstage with Jagger, Bowie, Mercury, and McCartney.

Afterwards he said, "I know you didn't Adam and Eve me but it was all true." He gave his shorter leg a hearty slap. "This old girl has never let me down."

"Your leg's a girl?" I said.

"Eileen," he said. "Get it?"

It took me a second. "Ha! Good one!"

He stood up to leave.

"Hey," I said. "Want to join our troupe?"

He grinned. "I thought you'd never ask."

CHAPTER TEN

The Royal St. John's Regatta was held on the first Wednesday of August, weather permitting. The night before, Mom and Dad played what the locals called Regatta Roulette—partying all night down on George Street hoping to God the next day would be a holiday. Mom wasn't sure she'd be up for it but Nan said it would do her and Dad good. They must have had a decent time because they stayed out real late. I know this because they made a racket coming home, laughing and knocking things over. Turns out, their gamble paid off. The next morning the sun was shining and the probability of precipitation was low. Mom and Dad went back to bed but

I headed down to Quidi Vidi Lake with a pocketful of coins and a boatload of excitement.

★

Saibal and I joined the crowds around the lake. The fixed-seat rowing races had already begun but we cared more about the games of chance. We went from stall to stall, throwing darts at balloons, gambling on the money wheels, and placing bets on Crown and Anchor. Our change was going fast but we were having a blast. With my last quarter, I bought a single ticket at the Knights of Columbus booth. It spun around and around, fast then slow. When it stopped, the man called the winner's number. "Five-zero-three!"

I looked at my ticket. Five-zero-three.

Saibal raised my hand into the air. "Over here! Over here!"

There were lots of stuffed toys to choose from. I picked a stuffed monkey.

"You okay?" said Saibal.

"Yes," I said. "I'm okay."

The food smells made our stomachs growl.

"I could eat the arse off a low-flying duck," said Saibal.

"Me too," I said.

We bumped into Pius. He bought us a plate of fish and chips with dressing and gravy.

"Ugh," said Saibal. "Freddie Fudge is here."

I looked around. "Where?"

Saibal pointed to a kid with spiky hair.

"He looks like a broom," I said.

"Who's Freddie Fudge?" asked Pius.

"Saibal's bully," I said.

"Finbar has a bully too," said Saibal.

"Don't worry, b'ys," said Pius. "Bullies always get their comeuppance."

Pius left us to eat our food by the bandstand. The CLB Band played "Up the Pond" and it filled me up.

"Look," I said. "It's that guy from *This Hour Has 22 Minutes*. The one who's always rantin' and ravin' at the camera."

"Rick Mercer," said Saibal. "Dad thinks he's a tool but Mudder thinks he's gorgeous."

"We could get his autograph for her," I said.

"Okay," said Saibal. "He can sign this empty container."

As we approached him I was struck with an amazing idea. "Instead of an autograph," I said, "we should ask him to lick the gravy. That way your mom will have his DNA."

"Brilliant," said Saibal.

Rick Mercer was in the middle of a conversation, but celebrities were used to getting interrupted, so I said, "Excuse me there, buddy. You wouldn't mind giving this gravy a lick, would ya?"

He looked at the congealed globs on the cardboard.

"My mom's a fan," said Saibal. "We'd like to give her some of your DNA."

"Oh, well in that case," said Rick Mercer.

He stuck out his tongue and dipped it in the gravy.

"Anything else?" he said. "You need a kidney or anything?"

"I have a question," I said. "Why are you always screamin' and bawlin' on TV?"

"A good rant is cathartic," he said.

"I'd love to get paid for shouting my opinions," said Saibal. "But I'm too brown for TV."

"You never know," he said. "Give it a few years and someone like you might be the star of *22 Minutes*."

"You really think so?" said Saibal.

Rick Mercer nodded. "I really do."

And with that, he walked away.

"Wow," I said. "Giving away DNA just like that. That man's a national treasure."

"He's a scholar and gentleman," said Saibal. "That's for sure."

We weaved our way through the crowds, watching kids on bouncy castles and riding ponies.

"We're too old for that stuff, aren't we, Finbar?" said Saibal.

"Indeed we are," I said.

We continued down the lakeside.

"Look," I said. "Coming out of the beer tent. It's the lead singer of Great Big Sea."

"Jesus," said Saibal. "Who are we gonna see next? Joey Smallwood?"

"Not unless he's rose from the dead," I said.

I cupped my hands around my mouth and yelled in the direction of the beer tent.

"Alan Doyle!"

When he looked over, I said, "Stay where you're to till we comes where you're at!"

A moment later, we were face to face.

"We'll be singing 'Goin' Up' at the talent show tonight," said Saibal.

Alan Doyle let out a laugh. "Will ye now?"

"We'll be dancing too," I said. "You should come watch."

"All right, b'ys," he said. "I'll see what I can do."

I held up the chip container. "Listen, me ol' trout. We're collecting celebrity DNA. Rick Mercer gave it a lick. We'd be honored if you did too."

Alan Doyle shoved his face in the container and dragged his tongue from one side of the cardboard to the other.

"Mmmm," he said. "Fee and chee with D and G. You can't beat it."

I wondered if he was drunk but rumor had it Alan Doyle was the happiest fella in Newfoundland.

As we walked away I said, "He could tell what we ate by the gravy."

"The man's a genius," said Saibal.

"Let's see who else we can find," I said.

"If we see Gordon Pinsent, I'll shit me pants," said Saibal.

"Nan would kill for some of his DNA," I said.

We spent another two hours at the regatta but saw no one else famous. We did find a five-dollar bill, though. We spent it on bouncy castles and pony rides.

★

We hid the chip container and the stuffed monkey in some bushes and went to the nursing home for a quick practice. Soon after, we were piling into the One Step Closer to God minibus. There were twenty-three of us all together, including Uneven Steven, the two musician fellas from the Harbour Light Centre, and an actual licensed minibus driver. Quidi Vidi Lake was a different place than it had been earlier. The stalls and stands were broken down and litter covered the ground. A stage had been erected downhill from the bandstand and a good-sized crowd sat on the hill facing it. At 6 p.m., the emcee took the stage. There were twelve acts in total, including Alfie Bragg and His Agony Bag and a dog named Upright who could walk on two legs. Both acts were big hits. Alfie's droning version of "Danny Boy" was powerful enough to bring a tear to a glass eye, and the two legs Upright could walk on were his front ones—no one saw that coming. As usual, the Full Tilt Dancers were standing-ovation amazing.

When the emcee announced our name—the Oldies but Goodies—a cheer erupted from the crowd. I followed the sound till I saw them. There they were, all five of them, sitting on the grass. Across Mom's lap was the Humpty Dumpty blanket. I swallowed a lump in my throat.

When the two fellas from the Harbour Light Centre started playing "Goin' Up," the crowd sang along. Everyone in Newfoundland knew Great Big Sea.

Our choreography was going as planned until Edie started a striptease. Thankfully she was having trouble with her buttons. Buster tried to distract the audience by twirling his cane. Old people, they've got no grip strength. Uneven Steven got it in the head. As he lay bleeding on the stage, Saibal executed his bhangra moves with extra oomph. The audience didn't know where to look. When Uneven Steven was taken off the stage, Alan Doyle hopped on. He strummed the hell out of his guitar. He didn't sing, he belted. We were lockin' the world outside, which was fine by me because who needs the world when you're havin' a time down at Quidi Vidi Lake.

Steven made it back onstage for the last few moments. He had a bandage on his forehead and blood dribbled down his cheek. When it came time for my solo, Alan Doyle said, "Take it away, me ol' trout." My pennies echoed all the way to Signal Hill. When the song ended, we didn't need a standing ovation because everyone was already on their feet.

Mom hugged me tight. Nan said I was a grand boy. Dad said it didn't matter if we won and I said, "But what about the money for SIDS?" Pius said, "It's the thought that counts." Shelagh placed her hands on her belly. There was a pain in my heart. It was sudden and strange and the ache was for her.

The audience was given ballots. Alan Doyle entertained the crowd by playing a few tunes with the Harbour Light fellas while the votes were being counted. Between songs Pius went up onstage and made an announcement. "Could Freddie Fudge please make his way to the stage? His prescription genital wart cream was found by the seniors' tent."

I looked over at Saibal, who was sitting on the hill with his parents. We laughed our arses off telepathically.

Alan Doyle played a few more tunes while we waited for the contest results. It was a good half hour before the emcee was back on the stage. The Oldies but Goodies gathered to hear the results.

"And the winner is . . ."

"I'm gonna piss myself," said Saibal.

"The Full Tilt Dancers."

I forced my hands together until they made a noise that sounded like clapping.

"I demand a recount," yelled Edie. "This election's been rigged."

I was starting to think her earlier visit to the porta-potty had been a trip to the beer tent instead.

Father O'Flaherty was presented with a giant check. He thanked the audience and said that the money had been intended for a new floor.

"Boo! Hiss!" yelled Edie.

He cleared his throat. "But it's come to my attention that there is a better, more deserving cause."

"Get off the stage, you old fool!"

"Edie. Shush!" I said.

"Finbar Squires, would you make your way to the stage?"

Saibal pushed me forward because I was frozen.

"Had the Oldies but Goodies won, this money would have been donated to SIDS research," said Father O'Flaherty. "The Full Tilt Dancers think this is a worthy cause and would like to present this check to the Squires family."

Father O'Flaherty shook my hand. I could barely look him in the eye.

"The anger," I whispered. "It's passing."

He passed me the check. "God bless you, Finbar."

I turned to the audience and held the check in triumph.

"One question," I said. "How am I going to fit this in the deposit envelope?"

The crowd laughed.

I jumped off the stage and grabbed Saibal. I picked him up and swung him around.

"This is the best day ever!"

Then I stopped.

Saibal hung in midair.

"You're allowed to be happy," he said.

I set him down. "Thanks, Saibal."

After a group hug with the Oldies but Goodies, Saibal ran to the bushes and got the chip container and the monkey. We brought the container to Steven.

"Will you give this a lick?" I said. "We're collecting celebrity spit."

"And seeing as you performed with the likes of Jagger," said Saibal.

Steven puffed out his chest. "I'd be honored."

He licked up a glob of gravy and grimaced.

"How's the ol' loaf of bread?" I asked.

He adjusted the bandage across his forehead. "I've got a bangin' headache, Squire. But I'll be all right."

Mom and Dad waved to us from the hill. Saibal and I joined them on the Humpty Dumpty blanket.

I sat next to Shelagh.

"Six hundred dollars," said Mom. "Wow."

The sun was going down over Quidi Vidi Lake. Ducks squabbled in the distance. A lone rower paddled toward the boathouse.

Dad looked at his watch. "We've been here two hours already."

Mom put her hand over the clock face. "Time slips away, love. Whether you count it or not."

"That it does," said Nan.

I put the stuffed monkey in Shelagh's lap.

"Here you go, Shelagh."

Pius laid a hand on my back.

"Gord would have liked the regatta," she said.

"Yes," I said. "He would have."

★

That night, only a few weeks after the first ruckus, there was another. Pius jumped out of bed. This time I followed.

Shelagh was standing in the hall, a puddle underneath her on the floor.

"God almighty," I said. "She's leaking!"

Mom shooed us away. "Go wake your father. Tell him to start the car."

Shelagh was as white as a ghost.

"Don't be scared," said Nan. "We've all been through it."

"I haven't," said Pius.

"I told you to go get your father!" said Mom.

"Barry," said Nan. "Grab some towels and wipe this up while we help Shelagh change."

"I'm not touching that," I said. "It came out of her hoo-ha."

"He needs another month," said Shelagh as she shuffled to her room. "He'll be too small."

"He?" I said.

Dad helped me clean up the puddle.

"Amniotic fluid," he said. "Isn't it wonderful?"

A pained shriek came from Shelagh's bedroom.

"Breathe," said Mom. "Breathe."

They bustled her down the stairs and out to the car.

"I can't do this," she cried.

Pius and I stood in the doorway.

"Good luck, Shelagh," I said.

Shelagh looked back. "Thanks, Barry."

★

We drank tea and ate a whole tin of shortbread.

"What time is it?" I asked every ten minutes.

Pius put on *Fawlty Towers* to pass the time. The sign outside the hotel said FLOWERY TWATS.

"What time is it?" I asked.

It was 6:23 a.m. when the phone rang. Pius answered.

"Wow," he said into the phone.

He hung up.

"It's a girl."

★

Dad drove us to the Health Sciences Centre. All around us, the world ticked along. People went about their business and I thought, "Don't they know? A baby was born today."

Everyone took turns holding her. I sat in a chair and waited. No one wanted to give her up.

When Pius placed her in my arms, he said, "She doesn't have a big schnoz at all."

Ten little fingers. Ten little toes. Cute little dimples where the knuckles should be.

I said, "You should call her Regatta."

They spoke at once, all five of them together.

"Shut up, Barry."

★

She was a month early but healthy as an ox.

A week later she was home.

I missed Gord.

I missed everything about him.

Saibal came. We stared at her while she slept.

She had spit bubbles on her lips.

He said, "It's not her fault."

I said, "I know."

★

I woke up. I'm not sure why. I went down the hall. Shelagh was sitting next to the crib, her hand in the slats.

"What if it happens again?" she said.

I sat beside her. "It won't."

She lay her head against the crib rails.

"Go back to bed, Shelagh," I said.

"I can't."

"I'll stay."

"You will?"

I nodded.

When she was gone, I put my hand through the rails.

"Hi, Molly."

I placed my finger on her palm. She closed her hand around it.

"Someday, when you're bigger, I'll take you out," I said. "Saibal will come with us. You'll like him and he'll like you. That's how it works. I'll take you to Caines and up Signal Hill. Someday I'll take you to the harbor and pretend to dump you in. Don't worry, you'll love it. Gord did."

★

I stayed with her till she cried to be nursed. Then I went to the basement. I pulled Gord's monkey sleepers down from the rafters. I added them to the dirty laundry and dumped the basket into the washing machine. I'd never done laundry before but it was pretty straightforward. I threw in some detergent, turned the dial to normal load, and hit Start. I put on Pius's hockey skates and worked on my Balance and Stability Training Academy 4 Real Dancers program, or BASTARD for short. When the laundry was done, I took off the skates and pulled the clean clothes into a basket.

Upstairs, I slipped on my shoes and went out on the back porch. The clothesline screeched through the pulley. I reached into the basket and pinned the items to the line: Dad's flannel shirt; my underwear with the hole in the arse; Mom's forget-me-not nightgown; Pius's hockey jersey; Nan's frilly shirt; Shelagh's wonder pants. I bent down and picked up Molly's sleepers. Out of the corner of my eye, I saw a shadow. I don't know how long she'd been watching. The sky darkened and the wind picked up. I looked to my mother and smiled.

"It's some day on clothes."

ACKNOWLEDGMENTS

Special thanks to Saibal Chakraburtty for helping me bring little Saibal into the world. I hope you are proud of your literary child. You should be. He's a whole lot like you.

To the Newfoundland actors, writers, comedians, and musicians who I have admired over the years: thank you for inspiring me with your humor, humility, warmth, and wit. Your skillful storytelling astounds me.

To the two celebrities who make cameo appearances in this book: you, sirs, are scholars and gentlemen. Thank you for (unwittingly) being a part of Barry's story.

To my editor, Lynne Missen: thank you for digging deep. Not only do you show me the holes in the story, you help smooth them over once they're filled in. You are a master.

To Peter Phillips, Sam Devotta, Vikki VanSickle, and all the fine people at Penguin Random House: thanks, me ol' trouts. Your enthusiasm and support is much appreciated.

To my agent, Amy Tompkins: it's nice to have someone rooting for you. Thanks for always being in my corner.

Finally, a shout-out to my family back in St. John's, whose hilarious shenanigans inspired the fictional Squires of York Street. Thanks for being half cracked.

In memory of Emily Louise Down.
October 5, 1987–December 20, 1987